Table of Contents

Introduction for Parents and Teachers

The Importance of Reading Classic Tales

Storytelling is an art that started long before stories were recorded and published. Orally passed from storyteller to storyteller in front of a crackling fire, many stories changed form, yet maintained similar plots and themes. We may credit these tales to names such as Jacob and Wilhelm Grimm, Charles Perrault, Joseph Jacobs, and Jørgensen and Moe, but in fact, these storytellers collected century-old stories from oral sources, crafted them, and wrote them down in the form we now enjoy.

Classic fairy tales and folk tales around the world are similar in their themes of good versus evil and intelligence or cleverness versus force or might. The details of the stories may change, but the themes remain universal.

Many fairy tales contain elements or suggestions of violence, such as the threat of being eaten by giants, witches, or ferocious wolves. In part, this violent bent emerged because early fairy tales were intended primarily for an adult audience, not for children. Fairies were often cast as the rich and powerful, with the main human character representing the poor, oppressed common person. The tales served as beacons of hope for the underprivileged in ancient times when there was little chance for social mobility.

Many psychologists today believe that fairy tales are good for children, because these tales represent what all people fear and desire, and thus help children face their own fears and wishes. Other psychologists say that children benefit from hearing stories with some element of danger, and then being reassured with happy endings in which the small, apparently powerless hero or heroine triumphs after all. This is especially true when a supportive parent takes the time to discuss the stories with his or her child and provide specific, personal reassurance.

Knowing classic stories and their characters will help ensure that your child begins to have a rich background in cultural literacy. Classic stories also expand the world of children by enriching their lives and empowering their learning. The tales present characters who undergo struggles and emerge transformed, thereby helping readers discover more about themselves. When your child identifies with these characters, he or she might better understand his or her own feelings and the feelings of other people.

Classic stories present diverse cultures, new ideas, and clever problem-solving. They use language in creative and colorful ways and serve as a springboard for your child's writing. Most of all, classic stories delight and entertain readers of all ages by providing the youngest reader with a solid base for a lifelong love of literature and reading.

Listen, Read, & Learn

With Classic Stories

Grade 3

Send all inquiries to:
School Specialty Publishing
8720 Orion Place
Columbus, OH 43240-2111

ISBN 0-7696-8353-3

2 3 4 5 6 7 8 9 10 POH 13 12 11 10 09

About This Book

Listen, Read, and Learn With Classic Stories has two main parts—the classic stories and the reading activities. The **classic stories** are a collection of fairy tales, fables, folk tales, rhymes, and legends. This collection may be read and reread regularly. Kindergartners and first graders will probably need some help reading the stories. Second and third graders should be able to read the stories more independently. When the book is finished, it can be saved as an anthology to begin or add to your child's home library.

Follow-up **reading activities** are included for each story to build your child's vocabulary and comprehension skills. These activities focus on skills such as phonics, word meaning, sequencing, main idea, cause and effect, and comparing and contrasting. Additional language arts activities center on grammar, punctuation, and writing. A unique feature to this book is that the activities are closely linked to the stories and not presented in isolation. They are taught within the context of the story. The benefit of this feature is a more meaningful learning experience.

Kindergartners and first graders will probably need help reading the directions, but children of this age should be able to complete the activities with a minimum of assistance. Second and third graders should be able to complete the activities more independently.

The activity pages are perforated for easy removal. There is also an **answer key** at the end of each book for immediate feedback.

A one-page **bibliography** at the end of each story is provided to guide you and your child to further reading. This list contains other tellings of the same story, usually one traditional and one with a twist, so your child can compare different approaches to the same story. Several enjoyable, age-appropriate books that are related in other ways to the story are provided as well. This list of books will come in handy during visits to the library.

A **reading skills checklist** on pages 295–296 can help you monitor your child's progress in reading comprehension. Of course, no two children progress at the same rate, but the checklist suggests appropriate reading goals for your child. Sample questions are listed for each skill. You may ask these before, during, or after reading to assess your child's ability to apply the skills.

At the end of the book you will find several pages of **everyday learning activities** you can do with your child in the subject areas of reading, writing, math, science, social studies, and arts and crafts. These activities will extend your child's learning beyond this book.

About "Rip Van Winkle"

Washington Irving was one of the first short story writers in American literature. His best-known short stories are "The Legend of Sleepy Hollow" and "Rip Van Winkle." Both stories were included in a collection of stories and essays Irving wrote in 1819–1820 called *The Sketch Book of Geoffrey Crayon, Gent.*

The tale of Rip Van Winkle is set in a Dutch settlement in New York State shortly before the American Revolution. The Dutch had first arrived in North America in 1609, sailing with the English explorer Henry Hudson. Within fifty years, New York was a major center for Dutch settlers.

Irving based his tale on a German folk tale. There was also a similar story told on Crete more than two thousand years earlier. The Greek author Diogenes Laërtius recorded this old story sometime around 200 A.D., but it had probably been passed along by word of mouth for several hundred years before that. In the Cretan tale, the father of a boy named Epimenides sends him into the field to look for a lost sheep. The boy lies down in a cave and sleeps for fifty-seven years. When he wakes up, he continues to look for the sheep, thinking he has taken only a short nap. Like Rip Van Winkle, Epimenides discovers the truth only when he returns home and finds everything changed.

Retold by Colleen Mulvenna

Rip Van Winkle

Illustrated by Francis Phillips

In the Catskill
Mountains in what is now the state of New
York, people tell many old legends about the
first Dutch settlers. In the mountains near the
Hudson River is a little village founded by
some of those first settlers. A simple, kind
man named Rip Van Winkle once lived in
this village, along with his wife and their
two small children, Rip and Judith.

The people of the village all loved Rip.
The children shouted a welcome whenever
he approached. Rip took part in their
games and told them stories. Whenever he
went walking, a group of children always
followed him, and not one dog in the village ever barked at him.

Rip was always willing to help his neighbors, but he rarely did any work around his own farm. His fences needed mending, and his cows were always wandering away. He seemed to grow more weeds than crops.

Rip's wife constantly scolded him for being lazy. So he spent most of his time with his friends at the village inn or wandering in the mountains.

One day when Rip got tired of his wife's nagging, he called his dog, Wolf, and went off toward the mountains. After walking a long way, he sat down on a grassy hill to enjoy the fine autumn day.

From where he was sitting, Rip could see the Hudson River and the thick forest. Before long, the mountains threw their long blue shadows over the village below. Rip knew that it would be dark long before he reached home. He heaved a deep sigh when he thought of what his wife would have to say to him.

Just as Rip was about to start on his way, he heard a voice in the distance. "Rip Van Winkle! Rip Van Winkle!" Rip looked around, but he saw nothing.

He thought his mind was playing tricks on him, and he began his long walk home. Again he heard the same voice crying out, "Rip Van Winkle! Rip Van Winkle!"

Wolf gave a suspicious growl and went to stand beside his master. Rip was frightened. He looked anxiously around again. An old man dressed in old-fashioned clothes was moving toward him. The man was bent under the weight of the barrel that he was carrying on his back. Rip, thinking that the man might need help, moved toward him.

The stranger was a short, squarely built old man. His hair was bushy and thick, and he had a full gray beard. The barrel he carried was full of cider, and it was almost as big as he was. He didn't say a word, but he made signs for Rip to help him with his load. Rip was uneasy, but he decided to help the man.

Every so often as they walked along, Rip heard a rumbling that sounded like distant thunder. Thunderstorms often occurred in the mountains, so he thought little of it and went on.

A short while later, Rip and the old man reached a grassy meadow. There Rip saw a group of short men playing ninepins. What an odd group they were! One had a long beard and small piggish eyes. Another had a face that was occupied entirely by his nose. All the men had beards of various shapes and lengths, and the longest belonged to the man who seemed to be in charge. He was a serious-looking gentleman with a weather-beaten face.

Rip realized that the thunder he had heard was the noise of rolling balls echoing through the mountains. When Rip and the old man got closer, the other men stopped their play and stared at Rip. Rip politely greeted everyone, but not one of the men said a word to him. Their staring made Rip so nervous that his knees began to knock together.

Rip's companion began to empty the contents of the barrel into large mugs. He made a sign that Rip should pass these mugs among the players. Rip, still uneasy, obeyed. The strange little men quickly drank down the cider in silence and returned to their game.

When Rip realized that the men did not mean any harm, he became less fearful. He even took a sip of cider when no one was looking. Rip found that he liked the taste of the strong cider, and he continued to steal sips. Soon he felt a little dizzy, and he fell into a deep sleep.

When Rip woke up, it was a beautiful morning. He found himself at the same spot where he had first seen the old man with the barrel. He rubbed his eyes. "Surely," said Rip aloud, "I have not slept here the whole night." He reached for his pocket watch, but it was not there.

Then he remembered the night before. He remembered the strange men, the game of ninepins, and the cider. "Now, what have I done?" said Rip. "What will I ever tell my wife? I cannot tell her about my adventure. She will never believe me."

He looked around for his watch, but he found only rusty bits and pieces of an old pocket watch lying on the ground. He suspected that the old men had stolen his. He decided to find them and demand that they return it.

Rip whistled for Wolf, but the dog did not come running. Rip started to get up and found that his joints were stiff. "These mountain beds do not agree with me," he mumbled. He began to look for the place where he had last seen the men playing ninepins.

Rip had a hard time retracing his steps. Trees seemed to have grown overnight because now they blocked his way. He couldn't find the grassy meadow where he had been the night before. He also began to feel very hungry. He decided he had better go home to face his wife. Again, he tried whistling for Wolf. When the dog still did not appear, Rip sadly started for home.

As he got close to the village, Rip saw a number of people, but he did not know any of them. This really surprised him. He thought he knew everyone in the village. As people passed Rip, they stared at him and stroked their chins. He finally touched his own chin and realized that his beard had grown a foot long!

Everything in the village was strange to Rip. He saw houses he had never seen before. He saw strange names over some doors. He didn't recognize the children who followed him, and strange dogs barked at him. Rip was very confused. He knew that this was the village he had left the day before, but somehow everything was different.

When Rip finally found his way to his small farm, he saw that it was deserted. The roof had fallen in, and the windows were broken. Inside he saw nothing but empty rooms.

Rip hurried back to find the village inn. Surely he would find his friends there, but the inn, too, was gone. In its place was a tall pole with a strange striped flag waving from it.

As Rip stared at the flag, a crowd of people gathered around him. One man began to ask him questions. "Tell me, sir, who are you? Where are you from?"

Rip didn't have the slightest idea what the man was talking about. Finally, he cried out, "Doesn't anybody here know Rip Van Winkle?"

"There he is, leaning against that post," said a man in the crowd.

Rip turned to look, and he saw a man who looked just like he had when he went up the mountain. This only confused him more. As the young man wandered over, Rip said, "I fell asleep in the mountains last night. When I woke up this morning, everything was different."

The people in the crowd all winked at one another. They thought Rip was crazy.

Then, a young woman with a crying baby in her arms joined the young Rip in the crowd. "Hush, Rip," she said to the baby. "The old man won't hurt you."

Rip was startled. "What is your name?" he asked.

"Judith Gardiner," was her reply.

"And your father's name?"

"Rip Van Winkle was his name, but it's been twenty years since he went away. His dog came home, but my brother and I have never seen our father since the day he walked off toward the mountains."

"What happened to your mother?" Rip asked.

"Oh, she has been dead for many years now."

Rip couldn't be quiet any longer. "I am your father!" he cried. "Doesn't anyone recognize me?"

Everyone in the crowd was amazed by Rip's words. Finally, an old woman in the crowd looked carefully at Rip and declared, "Sure enough, it is Rip Van Winkle! Welcome home, old neighbor. Where have you been these past twenty years?"

Soon, Rip had told his story. The twenty years had passed as if they had been only one night. Some people believed him, but most others still thought he was crazy.

Rip's daughter, Judith, took him to the comfortable home she shared with her husband. There he lived with her and her family.

Rip went back to taking long walks, playing with children, and talking with friends. And today, whenever thunder rolls through the Catskill Mountains, people think of strange little men playing a game of ninepins.

Bibliography
"Rip Van Winkle"

Moses, Will. *Rip Van Winkle*. New York: Philomel Books, 1999. This is a faithful retelling in simplified language, illustrated with oil paintings that have a folk-art look reminiscent of the artist's great-grandmother Grandma Moses.

Kittler, Robert. *Can't Sleep Count Sheep*. Longmont, CO: Count Sheep Publishing, 1998. Rip Van Winkle certainly had no trouble sleeping, but what do you do when you can't fall asleep? You might try reading this book of poems, but it will probably keep you awake laughing.

Wood, Audrey. *Sweet Dream Pie*. New York: Scholastic, 1998. Pa Brindle can't get to sleep without a slice of Sweet Dream Pie. Strange things happen, though, when Ma Brindle makes enough pie for everyone in the neighborhood.

Harshman, Marc. *All the Way to Morning*. New York: Marshall Cavendish, 1999. What kinds of sounds do children around the world hear as they fall asleep at night? A father and son on a camping trip listen to the katydids, and the father tells his son about different noises heard in various parts of the world. The book also shows a small map to help pinpoint each location.

Swain, Ruth Freeman. *Bedtime!* New York: Holiday House, 1999. Who would believe beds could be so interesting? This book details various types of beds, from the wooden frames with mosquito netting of ancient Egypt to the sleeping restraints of astronauts. Cat Bowman Smith's usual exuberant style of illustration makes this a decidedly un-sleepy book.

What a Character!

The story tells many things about Rip Van Winkle. Use the words from the word box to complete the sentences.

kindness	lazy
nervous	confused
loveable	simple

1. Rip Van Winkle was not a very serious man. He lived a rather

   _____ life.

2. Rip showed much _____ to his neighbors

   because he was always willing to help them.

3. Around his own home, though, Rip was

   _____ and didn't do much work.

4. The village people were always glad to see Rip Van Winkle

   because they found him sweet and _____.

5. When Rip was with the strange men playing ninepins, he felt

   uneasy and _____.

6. When Rip woke up, he didn't realized he'd slept so long. He

   was _____ when nothing looked the same.

Comprehension/Characterization   Listen, Read, and Learn With Classic Stories, Grade 3

Tell Me Again

Cut out the pictures here and on page 43. Put the story cards in order. Number them from 1 to 8. Then, glue each picture to a half sheet of construction paper. On each page, write what is happening in the story to describe the picture. Now, you have your own mini-book.

Rip Van Winkle

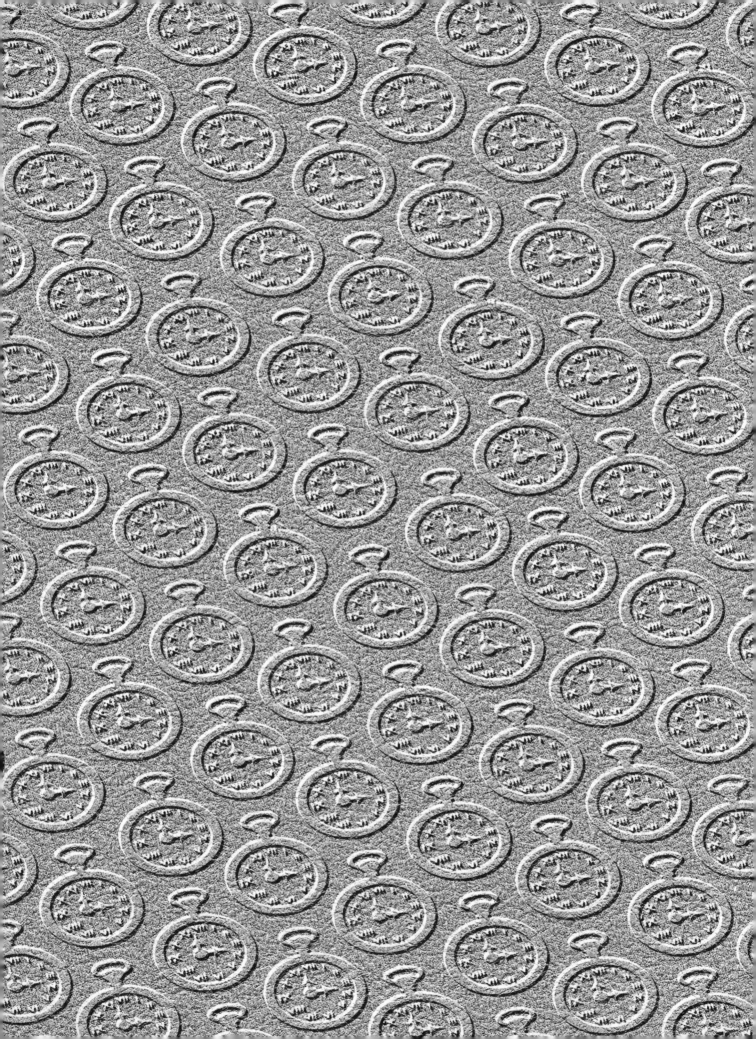

Rip Van
Winkle

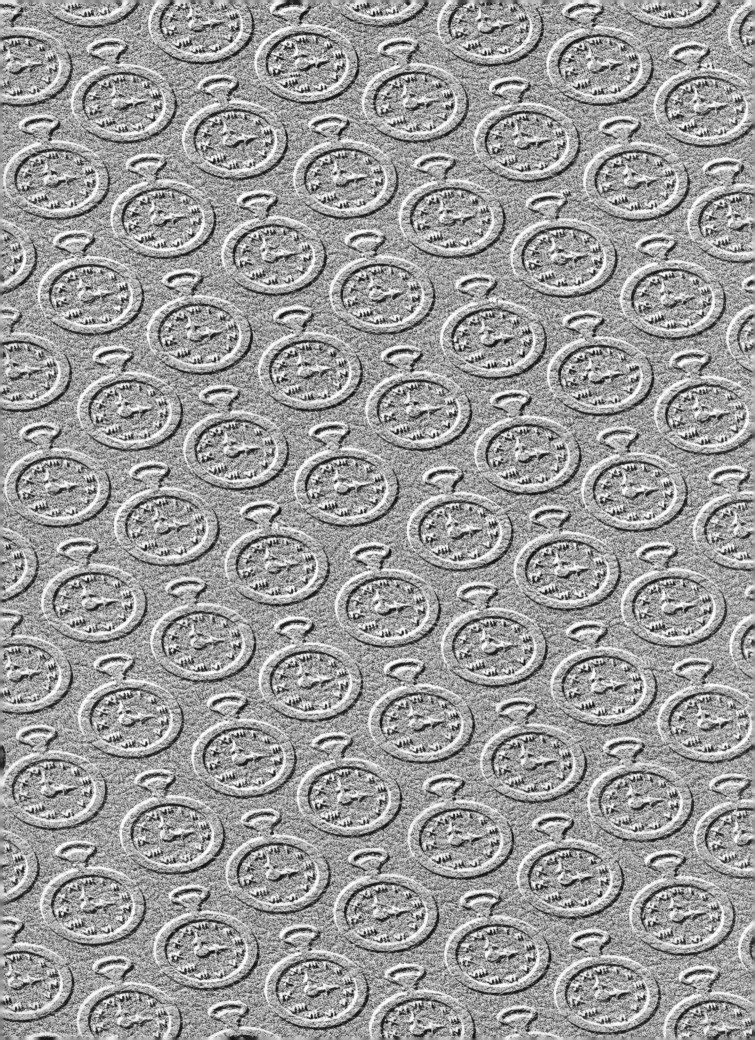

Plot It Out

The **plot** is what happens in a story. Use the chart below to record the plot of "Rip Van Winkle." Then, use the events to summarize the main thing that happens in the story. Make the summary only one or two sentences long.

Rip Van Winkle

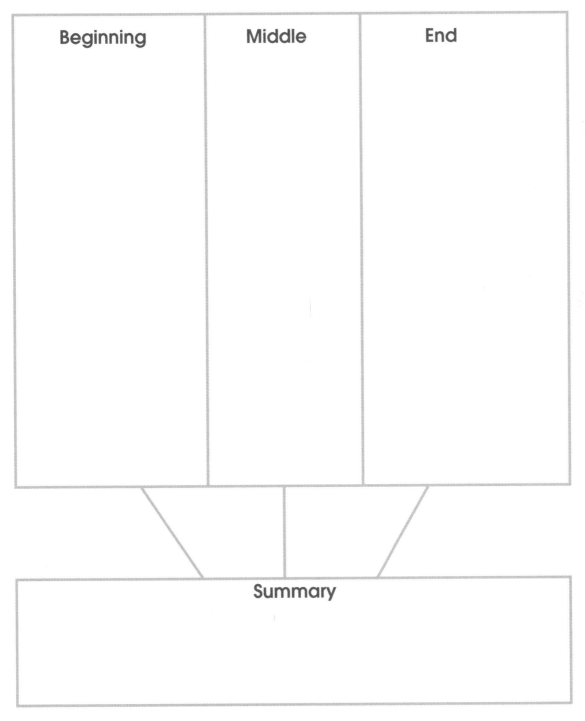

Beginning	Middle	End

Summary

A Place in Time

The **setting** is the place and time in which a story happens. Think about the setting of "Rip Van Winkle." Read each question below and answer it by writing **yes** or **no**. Then, write a brief description of the setting of "Rip Van Winkle."

Rip Van Winkle

1. Does the story take place in modern times? _____

2. Does the story take place in what is now the state of Florida? _____

3. Does the story take place in the mountains? _____

4. Does the story take place in a large city? _____

   The story "Rip Van Winkle" takes place _____

   _____

   _____

   _____

Comprehension/Setting

Listen, Read, and Learn With Classic Stories, Grade 3

More Confusion

Read each sentence. Underline one word in each sentence that makes the sentence not true. Change the sentence by replacing the underlined word with a word from the list. Write the new sentence.

thunderstorm   years   mountains   village   watch

Rip Van Winkle

1. The legend of Rip Van Winkle takes place long ago in the desert near the Hudson River. _____

_____

2. When Rip walked through the mountains with the strange man, he heard rumbling he thought was an earthquake.

_____

_____

3. When Rip woke up, he reached for his money, but only found rusted bits of metal. _____

_____

4. As Rip returned to the library, he found people were staring at him. _____

_____

5. After talking to people, Rip discovered that twenty minutes had passed for him as if they had been one night.

_____

_____

What's It All About?

Reread the introduction to "Rip Van Winkle" on page 6.
Think about what each paragraph is mostly about.
Then, read and circle the answer to each question below.

1. Which of these statements best tells the main idea of the first paragraph on page 6?

   Washington Irving wrote short stories, including "Rip Van Winkle."

   Washington Irving lived in the 1800s.

   Washington Irving's stories are part of American literature.

2. Which of these statements best tells the main idea of the second paragraph on page 6?

   Henry Hudson was an English explorer.

   New York was important for Dutch settlers.

   "Rip Van Winkle" takes place in a Dutch settlement in New York just before the American Revolution.

3. Which of these statements best tells the main idea of the last paragraph on page 6?

   A boy sleeps in a cave for 57 years.

   The story of "Rip Van Winkle" is like a story told on Crete.

   A boy looks for sheep after a nap.

4. What is another good title for page 6?

   _____

   _____

Reality or Fantasy?

When story events could really happen, they are called **reality**.
When story events could not really happen, they are called
fantasy. Read the following story events from "Rip Van Winkle"
and think about whether or not they could really happen.
Write each event in the correct place on the chart.

- Rip Van Winkle fell asleep in the mountains.
- Rip Van Winkle heard thunder that was really men playing ninepins.
- Rip Van Winkle slept for twenty years.
- Rip Van Winkle grew old.
- Rip Van Winkle returned to his village.

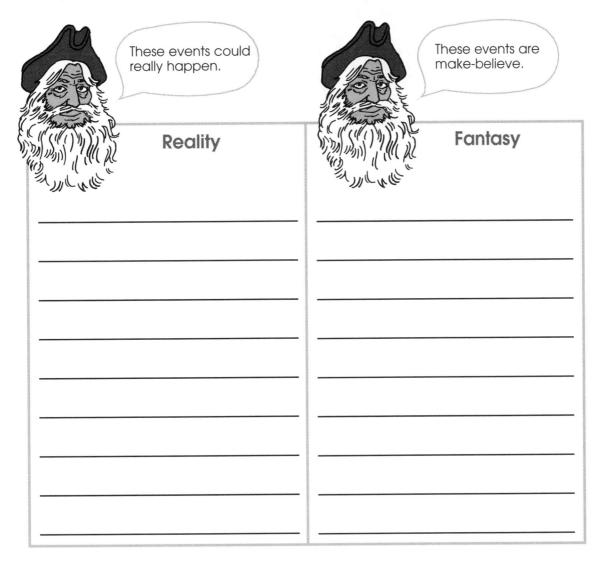

These events could really happen.

These events are make-believe.

Reality

Fantasy

Rip Van Winkle

Interesting Actions

Verbs are words that show action. Some verbs are more exact and give the reader more information. Read the following examples. Notice that a more exact verb is used in the second sentence.

Rip Van Winkle <u>looked</u> at the strange man.

Rip Van Winkle <u>gazed</u> at the strange man.

Read the following sentences. Replace the underlined verb with one that is more exact. Write it in the blank. Several answers are possible.

1. Rip <u>walked</u> in the mountains.

2. Wolf <u>ran</u> to Rip.

3. "You are so lazy!" Rip's wife <u>said</u>.

4. Rip <u>drank</u> some cider.

5. Rip <u>looked</u> for his watch.

6. When Rip returned to the village, he <u>told</u> his story.

What Is the Meaning of This?

Read each sentence. Choose the correct meaning of the underlined word. Circle the answer.

1. "Rip Van Winkle" is a <u>legend</u> set in a Dutch settlement.

   tradition   tale   time

2. The people of the <u>village</u> all loved Rip Van Winkle.

   community   club   café

3. Rip's wife would often <u>scold</u> him.

   offend   nag   promise

4. Rip's strange <u>companion</u> filled his mug with cider.

   pitcher of drink   enemy   a friend or person someone is with

5. When Rip returned to his farm, it was <u>deserted</u>.

   hot and dry   empty   just as before

6. One woman in the crowd <u>declared</u> that she recognized Rip.

   asked   wondered   stated

Rip's Journal Entry

Think about Rip Van Winkle's experience when he came back from the mountains. Complete the following sentences as if you are Rip Van Winkle writing a journal entry.

I can't understand_____.

The whole experience is unbelievable. I wonder about

_____.

Why did twenty years pass as one night?

When I went back to the village, I felt_____

_____. I was shocked

that _____.

I was sad that _____.

Of course, I didn't know I had been gone twenty years. Finally,

_____.

All the rest of my days I will _____

_____. Now I am happy to

_____.

Rip Van Winkle

People and Places

Words that name people, places, or things are **nouns**. Words that name special people, places, or things are **proper nouns**. Proper nouns begin with capital letters. Read these examples.

Black Hills

the Great Lakes

George Washington Carver

Find the proper noun in each sentence. Rewrite it with one or more capital letters.

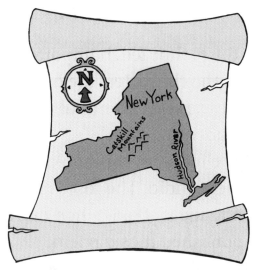

1. Long ago, settlers came to the catskill mountains.

   _____

2. The settlers were dutch people. _____

3. The settlers founded a village near the hudson river.

   _____

4. The area is now in the state of new york. _____

5. There is a story about a man named rip van winkle.

   _____

6. This man had a pet dog named wolf. _____

7. At the end of the story, the man finds his daughter, judith

   gardiner. _____

About Fables

Fables are stories that teach important lessons. Usually they are quite short, and often the characters are animals that think, speak, and act like people. Fables always have a moral, or lesson, which may be stated or may be left for the reader to decide.

The first of the fables in this book, "The Blind Men and the Elephant," was told in ancient India. The fable made its earliest known appearance in the English language in 1865, when an American poet named John Godfrey Saxe published it as a poem.

The other two fables are from Aesop, perhaps the best-known of all storytellers. It is believed that Aesop lived on a Greek island around 600 B.C. According to legend, Aesop was a strange-looking man, but he had a wonderful talent for telling stories that helped listeners discover important things about how to act. Aesop's fables were not written down until about 200 years after his death. Various writers recorded his fables, sometimes adding tales of their own to the collection. Even now, we enjoy the clever, humorous stories that he created, and we can learn from their wise lessons, which still apply today.

Retold by Mary F. Porsche

Fables

Illustrated by Robert Masheris

The Blind Men
and the Elephant

Long ago in a land of scorching
sun and tall palm trees, six blind
men made their home. They had
never seen trees or birds or clouds.
But blindness did not keep them
from enjoying the beauty around
them. A nightingale's sweet song,
the softness of sheep's wool, the
aroma and flavor of a spicy stew—
all these brought them pleasure.

One day a royal messenger arrived
from the city with wonderful news.
"The prince has received a gift from a
neighboring kingdom," the messenger
informed the villagers. "An elephant
has come to live at the palace."

Everyone was excited about this
event. There were no elephants in
their village, so they had no idea
what these animals were like.

"I have an idea!" Sashi exclaimed. "Let's travel to the city to meet the prince's elephant."

"Good thinking!" cried Pembro. "Each of us can touch it. Then, we will know what kind of animal an elephant is."

With much lively chatter, the six friends made plans for the long journey.

The next morning as the first rays of light appeared, the six men set out for the city. Higher and higher the sun climbed in the sky. Hotter and hotter the road felt beneath their feet. Hour after hour the tired travelers trudged on.

At last, the blind men reached the city. They trembled with excitement as they approached the palace.

"How big do you think an elephant is?" Raju wondered.

"Will it have a coat of soft fur?" asked Sashi.

"Perhaps elephants have thick, bushy tails," Pembro said.

A palace guard stopped the tiny band of travelers at the gate.

"A messenger told us that the prince has a new elephant," said Pembro.

"We have heard of elephants," Matmu said, "but we have never met one."

"If you will allow us to touch it, we can find out what an elephant is like," Tuni said.

"Very well," the guard agreed. "The prince is a fair and kind ruler. Certainly, he would not mind if you touch his elephant." With that, he led the six companions through the garden to the place where the elephant stood.

One by one, the men drew near the creature. Each one used his hands to find out what an elephant is like.

Raju was the first to approach the elephant. He put both hands against the animal's sturdy side. It did not move. He felt smooth, leathery skin as high and as wide as he could reach. "An elephant is like a wall," Raju thought.

Sashi ran eagerly toward the unfamiliar creature. He held the elephant's trunk and felt its curling, twisting motion. "An elephant is much like a squirmy snake," he decided.

Matmu was next to investigate this new beast. He ran his hands along a smooth, cool, ivory tusk. When he felt its pointed tip, he thought, "An elephant is like a spear."

Being the shortest of the six friends, Valto ran straight into one of the elephant's strong legs. He stretched his arms wide, but he could not even reach all the way around it. "An elephant is like the trunk of a tree," he decided.

As Tuni drew near to the animal, a slight breeze stirred the still, hot afternoon air. Just then, the blind man felt the gentle flapping of the elephant's huge ear. "What a surprise!" Tuni thought. "An elephant is like a fan!"

As it happened, Pembro felt the long, slender tail of the elephant swinging from side to side. "I think an elephant is like a rope," he decided.

Later, as they rested in the shade, the six friends began to talk about the elephant.

"I never guessed that an elephant would be like a wall," said Raju.

"What do you mean, a wall?" Sashi interrupted. "That elephant twisted and squirmed like a snake."

"That creature is no snake!" Matmu exclaimed. "It feels just like the sharpest of spears."

"That is ridiculous!" Valto chimed in. "A spear is thin and very light. The elephant is stout and very heavy. The animal is like the trunk of a tree."

"That cannot be!" said Tuni. "I felt it flapping in the breeze. An elephant is like a fan."

"You are all mistaken," Pembro said. "An elephant is like a rope that swings back and forth, back and forth."

Their voices grew louder and louder as the argument became more and more heated.
All at once, a horse galloped into the garden. The six blind men did not even hear the prince arrive. He dismounted and slowly walked over to the place where they were sitting. For a few moments, the prince listened carefully. Then, he spoke with a commanding voice.

"Quiet! What is all the commotion about?"

The friends suddenly became silent. Raju spoke first. "We came here to find out what an elephant looks like, but it is still a mystery."

"We are baffled," Sashi said. "All of us touched the same animal, but each of us describes him quite differently."

The prince replied calmly, "The elephant is a huge animal.

Its side is like a wall.

Its trunk is like a snake.

Its tusk is like a spear.

Its leg is like a tree trunk.

Its ear is like a fan.

Its tail is like a rope.

All of you are right. But you are all wrong, as well."

"Each of you has only a part of the story," the prince continued. "When you put all the parts together, only then will you know what an elephant is really like."

The words spoken by the prince made sense to the blind men. They learned much that day. They learned what an elephant was, and they learned that their prince was truly a wise ruler.

The Dog and His Bone

Pup pranced along the path through the woods, his head held high. The day was warm and sunny. Pup had had a wonderful morning, romping and playing with his friends. Now, he was headed home with a tasty bone for supper.

Never had the sky seemed so bright and the forest so beautiful.

"I am so hungry," Pup thought. "Now, I only have to make it across the river and around the bend in the road. Then, I'll be back in my own front yard. What a feast I'll have with this yummy bone!"

By and by, Pup came to the edge of the river. As he started across the bridge, he peered at the water below. The little dog stared at the calm surface of the stream.

"Look at that strange dog," Pup thought.

At first he wasn't sure what to make of all this. The unknown creature frightened him. Then, Pup noticed that the other dog seemed to greet him with a friendly wag of his tail. Feeling a bit braver now, Pup watched the dog in the river staring back at him.

"That dog has a bone, too," Pup thought. "In fact, his bone looks even bigger than the one I have. If I am clever and move quickly, I can snatch the bone he is holding. Then, I will have both his and mine."

Pup leaped forward suddenly. As he opened his mouth to grab the other dog's bone, the one he was holding fell into the water. Ker-splash!

Only then did Pup realize that there was no other dog. He had been looking at his own reflection in the stream.

"Oh, no!" groaned Pup. "My bone is sinking to the bottom of the river." Disappointed, and still hungry, Pup trotted off toward home.

Those who are greedy and want what others have often lose everything they already own.

The Milkmaid
and Her Pail

Molly was a farmer's daughter. Every morning as the sun rose, Molly set out toward the barnyard to begin her chores. Milking the cows was always her first task. Then, she carried her pail full of fresh milk to sell at the market.

One fine day, Molly milked the cows as usual. She left the barn and hurried along the path, balancing the full pail on her head. The sun was bright, and the breeze was cool. The air was filled with the sweet scent of the spring blossoms in the meadow.

"Every day I carry this heavy pail of milk into town," the milkmaid thought. "At the market I am paid a few pennies for my trouble. If only there were some way to earn even more money."

Molly continued along the path, thinking and walking, walking and thinking. Suddenly, a sweet birdsong floated down from the treetops, breaking in on her thoughts.

Molly spotted a canary perched on an elm branch. The tiny bird had feathers the color of pale yellow buttercups. Suddenly, Molly smiled.

"I know," Molly said, talking aloud to the canary. "Instead of selling my milk at the market, I'll churn it into golden butter. I can then sell the butter at a higher price than the milk alone would bring."

The girl became more and more excited as her plan began to take shape. "After selling the butter, I'll have money to buy a lot of eggs," Molly figured. "Then, I will no longer be just a milkmaid. When my eggs hatch, I'll feed the chicks with grain until they are fine and plump. With the money I earn selling chickens at the market, I'll buy a stylish dress and a pretty new hat."

The milkmaid pictured herself at the village dance, dressed in her beautiful new clothes. She giggled as she thought how envious all the other girls would be. With that, Molly tossed her head, and the milk pail tumbled to the ground.

"Oh, oh, oh," wailed the girl. "All the milk is lost."
It was impossible to save any of the milk as it spilled onto the path. So instead of earning a few pennies for her milk, Molly went home empty-handed. Now, she could not buy eggs. Her wild dreams of fancy clothes seemed like foolishness now.

"How much did you earn at market today?" asked Molly's mother when the girl returned to the cottage.

With shame, Molly explained that she had sold nothing that day because she was paying more attention to her plans than her steps.

Molly's mother, being very wise and understanding, responded calmly. "You may have come home without money today, but you have learned a valuable lesson, daughter. Never count your chickens before they are hatched."

Bibliography
Fables

Aesop. *Aesop's Fables*. Retold by Robert Piumini and illustrated by Fulvio Testa. New York: Barrons, 1989. There are many lessons to be learned in Aesop's fables. This collection includes some old favorites as well as some less-familiar fables, such as "The Fox and the Stork" and "The Old Lion and the Fox."

Aesop. *Aesop's Fables*. Seattle: University of Washington Press, 1997. This collection of some of the most popular fables of Aesop, illustrated by the noted African-American artist Jacob Lawrence, includes in the introduction a brief explanation of the origins and development of Aesop's fables.

Aesop. *The Fox and the Rooster: A Fable from Aesop*. Retold by Charles Santore. New York: Random House, 1998. A hungry fox has plans for a rooster he spots at the top of a tree, but the rooster comes up with a plan of his own.

Backstein, Karen. *The Blind Men and the Elephant*. New York: Scholastic, 1992. This is an entertaining retelling of the fable of the six blind men with their very different ideas of what an elephant is.

Demi. *One Grain of Rice: A Mathematical Folktale*. New York: Scholastic, 1997. When a greedy raja keeps all the rice in his kingdom, refusing to share with the people in time of famine, a clever village girl named Rami asks for one grain of rice, doubled each day for thirty days. Soon there is more than enough rice to feed her village, and the raja learns a lesson in generosity. Demi's illustrations, inspired by Indian miniatures, are both beautiful and humorous.

What's the Point?

Fables

A **fable** is a story that teaches a lesson. Complete the chart by writing a summary of what happens in each story. Then, choose the lesson from the list below that fits the story. Write the letter of the lesson in the last column. Not all the choices will be used.

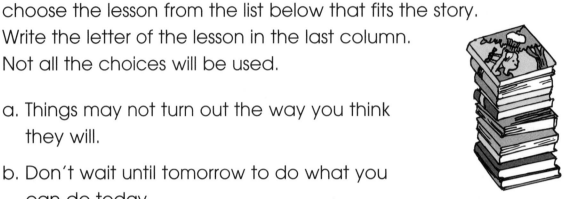

a. Things may not turn out the way you think they will.

b. Don't wait until tomorrow to do what you can do today.

c. You have to put all the parts of the story together to get the whole story.

d. In times of trouble, use your head to find a solution to the problem.

e. Don't lose everything you have because you wish for what others have.

Title	Summary	Lesson
1. The Blind Men and the Elephant		
2. The Dog and His Bone		
3. The Milkmaid and Her Pail		

Comprehension/Summarizing   Listen, Read, and Learn With Classic Stories, Grade 3

Front-Page News

Fables

Picture yourself as a reporter. Imagine that you have interviewed one or more of the blind men, Pup, or Molly the milkmaid. Write a news article based on the facts you have gathered.

1. Record your interview notes on the notebook page below.

2. Write your story on a separate sheet of paper. Give details that tell who, what, when, where, and why.

3. Draw a picture that shows an important event in the story.

Notes

Words to Watch

Read each meaning. Find a word from the box that matches the meaning. Write the word on the line.

pranced	scorching	blossoms
peered	task	reflection
trudged	valuable	commotion

1. extremely hot

   _____

2. walked slowly as with difficulty

   _____

3. a lot of excitement

   _____

4. walked in a lively way

   _____

5. looked at carefully

   _____

6. an image formed

   _____

7. a job

   _____

8. worth much

   _____

9. blooms on flowers

   _____

Fables

Character Forecast

When you **predict** what a character might do or what might happen next in a story, you use clues from what you've read. Make a prediction about each fable. Read the question and circle the best answer. Then, list the clues you used from the story to make the prediction.

1. What do you think Pup will do the next time he sees something he'd like to have?
   a. try to get it away from the owner
   b. appreciate what he has
   c. go to sleep

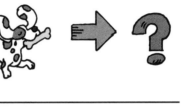

Clues: _____

_____

2. What do you think Molly the milkmaid will do the next time she makes plans about the future?
   a. pay attention to what she is doing at the time so her plans are not spoiled
   b. tell everyone she knows about her plans because she is sure they will happen
   c. worry about her plans until they happen

Clues:_____

_____

3. What do you think the blind men will do the next time they explore something new?
   a. explore just one part of the thing
   b. choose one of them to do all the exploring
   c. make sure they think about all the parts instead of just one

Clues:_____

_____

Comparing Elephants

The blind men in the fable learned about the elephant by touching it. They might have been surprised to find out that not all elephants are the same. There are two types of elephants: African elephants and Indian elephants. Study the picture diagrams to compare them. Then, use the Venn diagram on page 231 to show ways these elephants are alike and ways they differ.

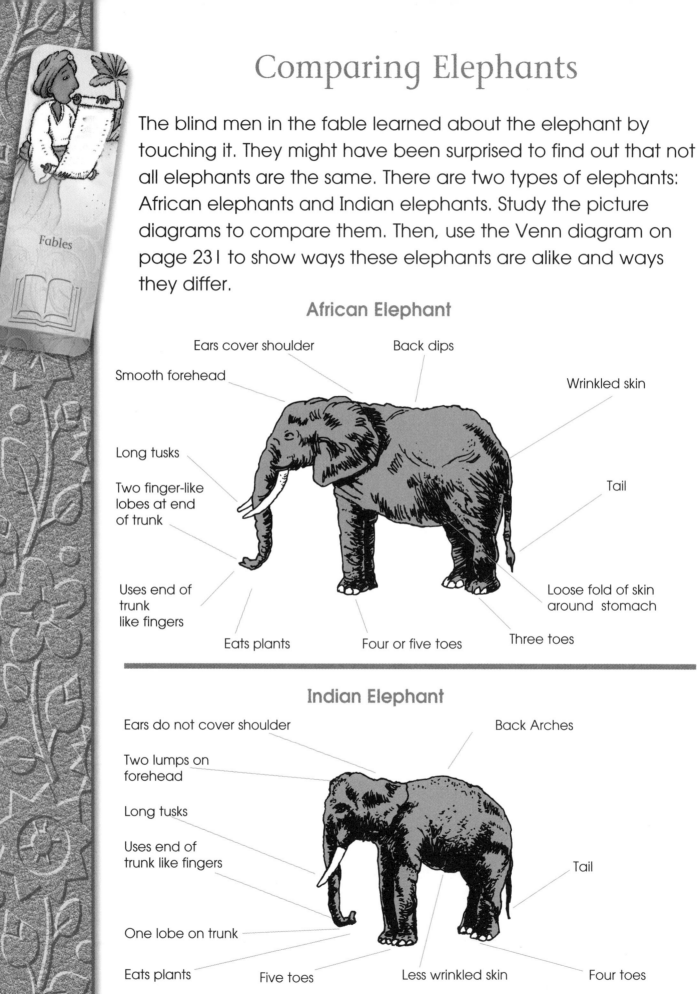

African Elephant

Ears cover shoulder

Back dips

Smooth forehead

Wrinkled skin

Long tusks

Two finger-like lobes at end of trunk

Tail

Uses end of trunk like fingers

Loose fold of skin around stomach

Eats plants

Four or five toes

Three toes

Indian Elephant

Ears do not cover shoulder

Back Arches

Two lumps on forehead

Long tusks

Uses end of trunk like fingers

Tail

One lobe on trunk

Eats plants

Five toes

Less wrinkled skin

Four toes

Comprehension/Compare and Contrast

Listen, Read, and Learn With Classic Stories, Grade 3

Fables

Comparing Elephants (page 2)

In the circle labeled African Elephant, list words that describe only the African elephant. In the circle labeled Indian Elephant, list words that describe only the Indian elephant. In the middle section labeled Both Elephants, list words that describe both kinds of elephants.

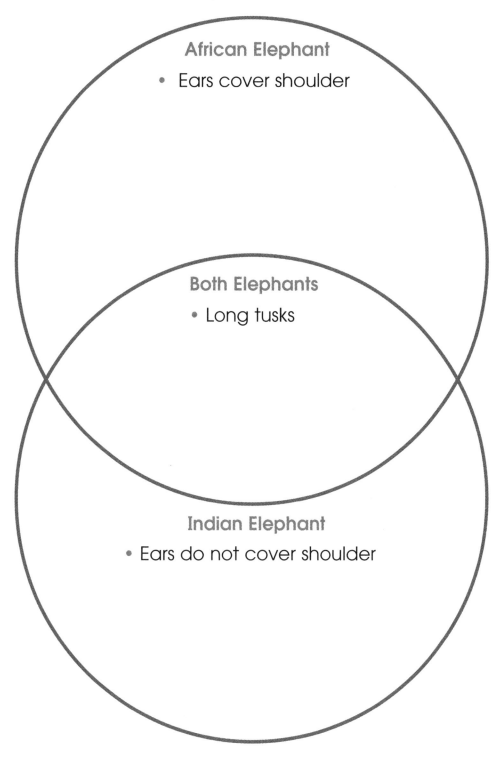

African Elephant

- Ears cover shoulder

Both Elephants

- Long tusks

Indian Elephant

- Ears do not cover shoulder

Announcing the Details

Fables

Read each sentence. If the sentence tells about something that happened in "The Blind Men and the Elephant," color the scroll green. If the sentence tells about something that did not happen in the story, color the scroll red.

The prince received a gift of an elephant.

The blind men traveled to the palace to meet the elephant.

The prince didn't allow the blind men to touch the elephant.

The blind men each touched a different part of the elephant.

The blind men all had the same thoughts about the elephant.

The elephant ran away from the blind men.

One of the blind men thought the elephant was like a wall.

One of the blind men thought the elephant was like a snake.

The blind men each made a sculpture of the elephant.

The prince explained to the blind men that they each had only part of the story.

Comprehension/Story Details   Listen, Read, and Learn With Classic Stories, Grade 3

Could It Really Happen?

Some events in a story can really happen. These things are called **reality**. Some events could not really happen. These things are called **fantasy**. Read each sentence. Circle **reality** or **fantasy** to show whether or not the event could really happen.

1. A dog walks through the woods.   Reality   Fantasy

2. A dog looks at his reflection in a river.   Reality   Fantasy

3. A dog says, "Look at that strange dog."   Reality   Fantasy

4. A dog wants to think of a clever plan to get another bone.   Reality   Fantasy

5. A dog thinks to himself that the sun looks brighter than ever.   Reality   Fantasy

6. A dog gets hungry.   Reality   Fantasy

7. A dog tries to take a bone home.   Reality   Fantasy

8. A dog leaps forward suddenly.   Reality   Fantasy

Pup's Time Line

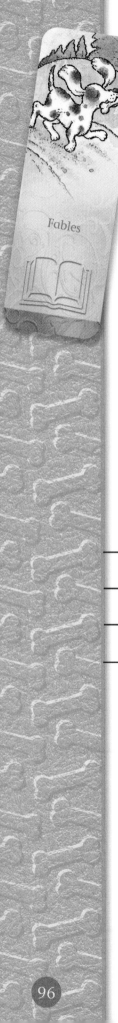

Read each event below.
Write the events in order
on the time line.

Events

Pup tried to snatch the dog's bone but lost his.

Pup came to the edge of the river.

Pup played with his friends.

Pup spotted another dog as he crossed the bridge.

Pup headed home with a bone to eat.

Pup realized that the other dog was his own reflection.

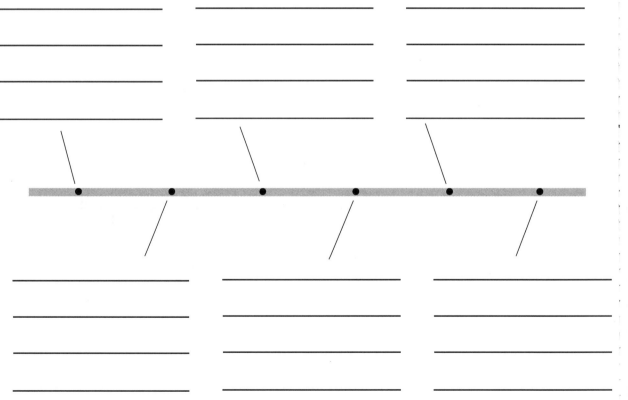

Comprehension/Sequencing

Milkmaid Traits

Think about the character Molly from "The Milkmaid and Her Pail." Choose three character traits from the box to complete the web.

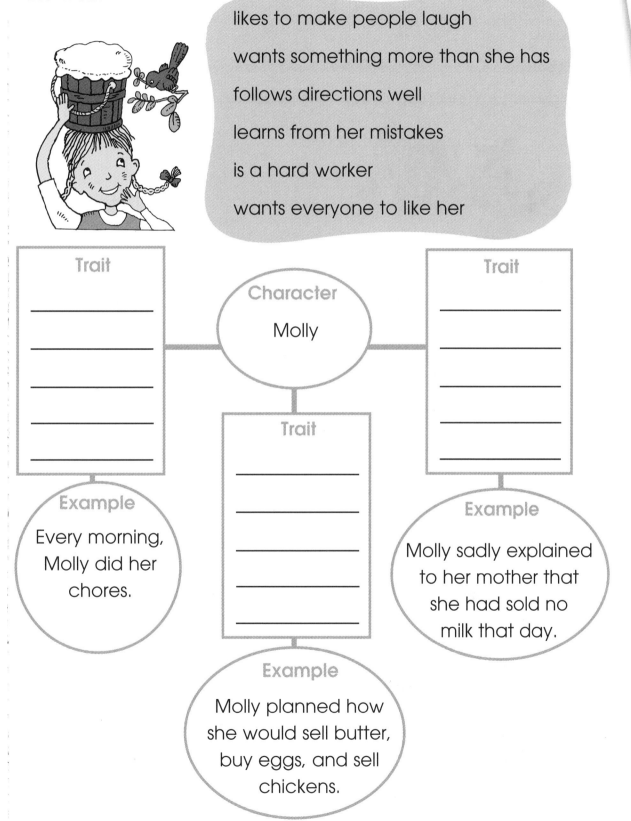

likes to make people laugh

wants something more than she has

follows directions well

learns from her mistakes

is a hard worker

wants everyone to like her

Fables

Trait

_____
_____
_____
_____

Character

Molly

Trait

_____
_____
_____
_____

Trait

_____
_____
_____
_____

Example

Every morning, Molly did her chores.

Example

Molly sadly explained to her mother that she had sold no milk that day.

Example

Molly planned how she would sell butter, buy eggs, and sell chickens.

What's Missing?

A **sentence** tells a complete thought. It includes a **naming part** and an **action part**. Read each sentence below. Either the naming part or the action part is missing. Write **naming** or **action** on the line to tell what is missing.

Example: Many of these stories happened a long time ago.

naming part   action part

What's missing?

1. touched the elephant   _____

2. the tiny band of travelers   _____

3. is like the trunk of a tree   _____

4. romped and played with his friends   _____

5. that very strange dog   _____

6. the completely unknown creature   _____

7. Molly the milkmaid   _____

8. floated down from the treetops,

   breaking in on her thoughts   _____

9. seemed like foolishness now   _____

Grammar/Complete Sentences   Listen, Read, and Learn With Classic Stories, Grade 3

Summarizing With Captions

A **caption** is text that tells information about a photo or illustration. Look at the illustrations on the following pages and skim the text. Circle the caption that best summarizes what the illustration shows.

Fables

Page 79

Molly is a happy girl.

Molly goes to milk the cow each day.

Molly has a cow.

Pages 80-81

Molly gets exercise every day.

Molly likes flowers.

Molly takes the milk to town to sell it.

Page 82

Molly gets an idea from a canary.

Molly is a pretty girl.

Molly carries the pail on her head.

Page 83

Molly is tired of carrying the milk.

Molly has grand plans for herself in fancy clothes.

Molly wants to go home.

Page 84

Molly thinks of a way to save the milk.

Molly is practicing her dance steps.

Molly is sad because she spilled the milk.

Page 85

Molly's mother tells her to sweep the cottage.

Molly explains to her mother what happened.

Molly and her mother have to move to a new cottage.

A Careful Reading

Read the following text that might appear on the book jackets of the fables. For each story, find and correct two capitalization mistakes, two punctuation mistakes, and two spelling mistakes. Make your corrections above each mistake or within the paragraph.

The Blind Men and the Elephant

what does an elefant look like. That is the question six men who are blind want to answer. To do so, they touch an elephant. the problem is, each touches a different part and has a different idea about what an elephant is like With help from a prince, the men figure out that they have to put all the parts together to get the complete store.

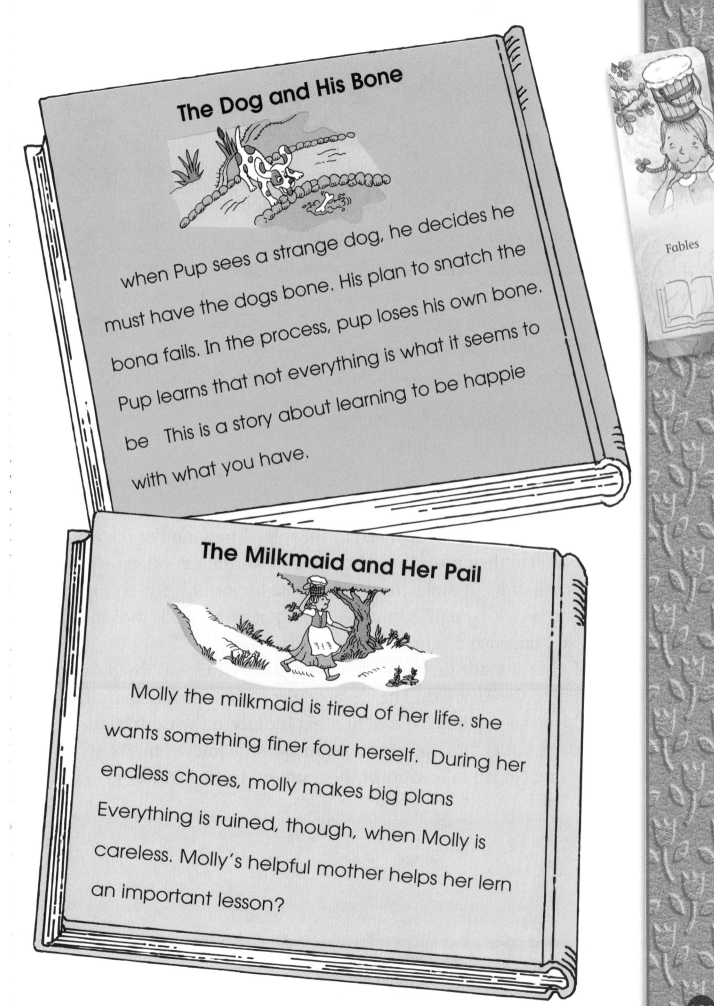

The Dog and His Bone

when Pup sees a strange dog, he decides he must have the dogs bone. His plan to snatch the bona fails. In the process, pup loses his own bone. Pup learns that not everything is what it seems to be This is a story about learning to be happie with what you have.

The Milkmaid and Her Pail

Molly the milkmaid is tired of her life. she wants something finer four herself. During her endless chores, molly makes big plans Everything is ruined, though, when Molly is careless. Molly's helpful mother helps her lern an important lesson?

Fables

About "The Anansi Tales"

Many stories first told in West Africa feature clever animals that talk and act like people. Often these characters are small, weak creatures that use their wit, and sometimes magic, to trick animals that are much bigger and stronger than they are. Storytellers wove the adventures of these characters into amusing tales that people still enjoy today.

One sly trickster is Anansi. At times, he is shown as a man. In many tales, however, Anansi is a spider. In fact, the word ananse means spider in the language of the Ashanti people, who lived on the West African coast. Mischievous and clever, Anansi gets what he wants by taking advantage of more powerful creatures. In times of danger, the tiny spider can escape to his web, well out of harm's way.

Sometimes African words are included in the tales. The sound of the words usually gives a clue to their meaning. Also, African storytellers often repeat words or phrases in order to make them seem more important. For example, the phrase "Long ago, long ago" at the beginning of a story tells that the events to be told happened a very long time ago.

The tales of Anansi made their way across the Atlantic Ocean when slaves were transported to the Americas. The clever spider is still a folk hero in the tales told by the people of Jamaica and of other islands in the Caribbean. Also, the character sometimes appears as Anancy in the tales of the West Indies, and as Aunt Nancy in folklore of the southern United States.

Retold by Mary F. Porsche

Anansi Learns to Fish

Illustrated by Donna Perrone

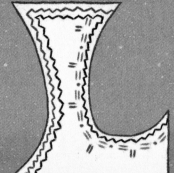ong ago, long ago in the villages of West Africa, the Ashanti people gathered around fires in the dark of night. Skilled storytellers wove tales that were told again and again, enjoyed by both young and old. The most famous of these tales are the "Spider Stories," which tell of a trickster named Anansi.

Now, sometimes this character is shown as a spider, and sometimes he appears as a man, and sometimes he is somewhere in between. He delights in acts of mischief and enjoys a good laugh at the expense of others. Often Anansi succeeds in getting the better of characters much bigger than himself. At times, however, his wit is no match for the cleverness of others, and Anansi plays the fool.

Late one afternoon by the river's edge, Anansi the Spider spotted his friend Turtle carrying a big fish. "Where did you get such a huge fish?" Anansi asked his friend.

"I caught it in the river," Turtle replied.

Now, Anansi loved to eat fish, but he was much too lazy to catch them. "Turtle is rather slow, and he isn't too bright," Anansi said to himself. "I'll ask Turtle to go fishing with me and trick him into doing all the work. Then, I will take all the fish for myself."

So Anansi said to his friend, "Will you show me how to catch fish?"

"Certainly," replied Turtle. "Come to the river tomorrow morning, and I will show you what to do. After all, two of us working together can catch twice as many fish as one of us working alone."

The next morning, Anansi and Turtle met on the bank of the river. "What a fine day for fishing!" Turtle exclaimed. "Let's get started."

"This will be as simple as making a hyena laugh," Anansi said to himself. His mouth began to water at the thought of all the fish that Turtle would be catching for him.

"First, we must gather vines to make a net," said Turtle. "The toughest, most flexible ones are found among the thorn trees. When I gather the vines, I work hard and get scratched. Since we are partners, we can share the task. One of us can work hard, and the other can get scratched."

"I have four arms and four legs," gasped Anansi. "I don't want to get scratched. I will work hard, work hard cutting the vines, while you get scratched."

So Anansi crawled bravely under the jungle bush in search of strong, supple vines. Meanwhile, Turtle made himself comfortable in the shade of the thorn trees and waited for his friend to return.

Several hours later, Anansi returned with many long vines that were just right for making fishing nets.

"Look, Turtle. Now we are ready to make a large fishing net."

"I can tell you have done a fine job, fine job," said Turtle. "I can feel the pain of the scratches. I must go home now and rest. Meet me here tomorrow, and we will make a fine fishing net."

At sunrise the next morning, Anansi was waiting for Turtle at the riverbank.

"Our next task is to make a net," said Turtle, "but net making isn't easy. Whenever I weave a net, I work and get tired. Let's do it together. One of us can work, and the other can get tired."

"Oh, I don't want to get tired!" Anansi cried. "I will work on the net, and you can get tired."

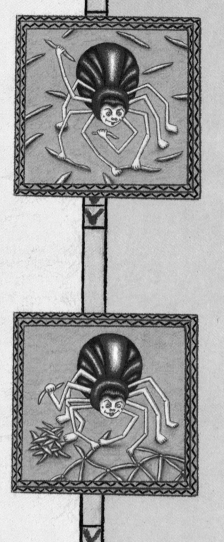

So Turtle showed his friend how to weave the vines and knot them to form a strong net. Then, he stretched out in the sun on the riverbank while Anansi continued his task.

By and by, Anansi said, "Weaving a net is hard work."

"I can tell that you are working hard, working hard," Turtle told Anansi, "because I am feeling very tired." Turtle became so tired while the spider worked that he drifted off to sleep.

Several hours later, Anansi awoke his friend. "The net is ready," said Anansi. "Now we can catch fish."

"You have done a fine job, fine job," said Turtle, "but you have worked so hard that I am exhausted. I must go home to bed. Come back tomorrow morning, and I will show you how to fish."

The next morning, Anansi again met Turtle at the river's edge. "Today we will set the net in the river," Turtle announced. "It isn't an easy job. Whenever I place a net, I work hard and get tired. Since you worked so hard yesterday, why don't I work today and let you get tired."

But Anansi wouldn't hear of this. "Getting tired is the hardest part. I'll set the net, Turtle, and you can get tired."

So Turtle settled down on the bank of the river.

The spider worked for hours, lifting and tugging, lifting and tugging the heavy net.

"I can tell that you are working hard," Turtle told Anansi, "because I am getting quite tired." Before long, Turtle was fast asleep.

When Anansi had set the net in just the right position in the river, he woke Turtle.

"We're ready to catch fish now, Turtle," Anansi said proudly.

"You have done a fine job, fine job," Turtle said yawning, "but I am so tired that I must go home and sleep. Meet me here tomorrow, and we will catch some fish."

Anansi arrived at the riverbank bright and early the next morning. "I can't wait to catch my first fish!" exclaimed the spider.

"Fishing is hard work," Turtle said. "Since you have worked hard for three days, perhaps you should let me catch fish while you get tired."

"No!" exclaimed Anansi. "I don't want to get tired. I'm going to catch a fish!"

"As you wish," Turtle said, and he settled down on the riverbank with his sketchpad. He was already feeling tired as Anansi started to work.

Again and again, Anansi struggled to pull in the net. The harder the spider worked, the more tired Turtle became. After hours of backbreaking work, Anansi finally discovered a big fish wriggling inside the net.

"Eee! Eee! Eee!" Anansi shrieked with delight as he did a little dance. Of course, the commotion awakened Turtle, who sat up and stretched his arms out wide.

"What happens next?" Anansi wanted to know.

"The fish must be cooked," said Turtle. "You have worked so hard, so hard, Anansi. Let me cook the fish while you get tired."

"Oh, no!" replied Anansi, who was planning to eat the whole fish by himself. "I will do the cooking."

So, as Turtle yawned and went back to sleep, Anansi started a fire. He grilled the fish until it was golden brown.

The wonderful aroma of cooked fish awakened turtle. "You are a good cook, Anansi. I can almost taste that fish. It's time to eat."

"When I am fishing alone," said Turtle, "I eat the fish and get full. Since we are a team, let's work together. One of us can eat, and the other can get full."

"I would rather get full," Anansi said quickly. So Turtle started eating, and Anansi sat nearby on a log, waiting for the hollow feeling inside him to fill up.

"Are you feeling full yet?" Turtle asked, after he had taken several bites.

"Not yet," Anansi said. So Turtle continued to eat.

A little while later, Turtle asked again, "Now are you beginning to get full?"

"I'm as hungry as ever," Anansi complained. "Eat some more."

"Are you full yet?" Turtle asked a third time.

"No, I don't feel one bit fuller than when you started."

"That's a shame," replied Turtle, "because there isn't any fish left."

When Anansi saw that Turtle had picked the fish bones clean, he realized then that he had been tricked. "This isn't fair!" Anansi screamed.

"What do you mean?" Turtle responded.

"You made me do all the work, and you ate all the fish," shouted Anansi. "You'll pay for this. I'm going to the Justice Tree."

*H*issing and fuming, Anansi scurried to the Justice Tree. Warthog was sitting nearby. Now, whenever the jungle animals had disagreements, they brought their troubles to Warthog. They knew that he was a wise and fair judge.

"Why are you here?" Warthog asked Anansi.

"Turtle cheated me," Anansi said. "When we went fishing, I did all the work. Then, he ate all the fish."

Now, Warthog knew that Anansi was a lazy creature who never worked hard at anything. "Tell me what you did, Anansi," commanded Warthog.

"I gathered vines, and I wove a net," said Anansi. "Then, I set it in the river. Again and again, I pulled the net up onto the riverbank. Finally, I caught a fish and cooked it over a fire."

"You must have been tired after all that work," Warthog said.

"Not at all," said Anansi. "Turtle and I were a team. I worked hard, and Turtle got tired."

131

"Turtle got tired?" Warthog was confused. "What did Turtle do?"

"Nothing," Anansi replied.

"You are talking nonsense. If Turtle got tired, he must have been doing all the work. I don't believe your ridiculous story. Go home and stay out of mischief."

Anansi knew that Warthog's decision was final. The outwitted spider made his way back home. He was ashamed that Turtle had made a fool of him. It was a long time, a long time, before he returned to the river. And he never talked to Turtle again.

Anansi did continue to use his skill for creating fine nets, though. He taught his friends how to weave the nets and how to use them to catch food. Today, these nets are known as "webs."

Bibliography
"Anansi Learns to Fish"

Kimmel, Eric. *Anansi Goes Fishing*. New York: Holiday House, 1993. This is one of several retellings of Anansi tales by Eric Kimmel. His lively text and Janet Stevens's clever art make this story one to read and reread.

Aardema, Verna. *Anansi Does the Impossible!: An Ashanti Tale*. New York: Atheneum, 1997. Long ago, all stories were owned by the sky god. Anansi set out to change that with the help of his clever wife, Aso. First, though, Anansi must perform three seemingly impossible tasks.

McDermott, Gerald. *Anansi the Spider: A Tale from the Ashanti*. New York: Henry Holt, 1988. When Anansi goes far from home and gets lost, his six sons—See Trouble, Road Builder, River Drinker, Game Skinner, Stone Thrower, and Cushion—come to the rescue!

Aardema, Verna. *Why Mosquitoes Buzz in People's Ears*. New York: Penguin Group, 1992. This tale, like the Anansi tales, is from West Africa. A jungle disaster is set off when Mosquito tells Iguana a tall tale. Iguana is so bothered being told such nonsense that he plugs his ears, and a delightfully mischievous chain reaction of mishaps begins!

Bryan, Ashley. *Beat the Story-Drum, Pum-Pum*. New York: Aladdin, 1987. As the title of this collection of five Nigerian folktales suggests, author/illustrator Ashley Bryan picks up on the rhythmic beat of the drum as he tells the tales. In addition, his colorful, vigorous woodcuts won him the 1981 Coretta Scott King Award for illustration. This award is presented annually to a black author and a black illustrator for an outstandingly inspirational and educational contribution.

Well Noted

Read the following note Turtle might have written to Anansi. Find and correct three capitalization mistakes, three punctuation mistakes, and two spelling mistakes. Insert the end punctuation where needed. Make the capitalization and spelling corrections above the type.

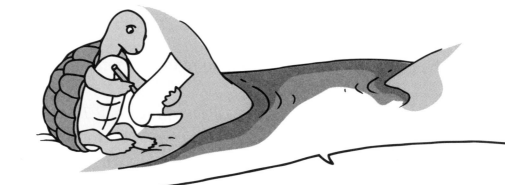

Dear anansi

i am sorry for what I have done. It wasn't very nice to trick you that waay. I would like to try again to be your friend. Would you please come over for dinner. I would like to cook some fish for you. it will make up for the one I ate without sharing If you could come for dinner, I think it would be fune.

Your friend,

Turtle

Grammar/Mechanics

Listen, Read, and Learn With Classic Stories, Grade 3

Anansi Takes the Stage

Make stick puppets to retell "Anansi Learns to Fish." Color the characters below, then cut them out. Use glue or tape to attach a craft stick or pencil to the back of each cutout. Use your puppets to act out the story.

Anansi Learns to Fish

What a Character!

Adjectives are words that describe nouns. An author often uses words such as **brave**, **truthful**, or **stingy** to describe a character. A character's actions also show what he or she is like. Choose words from the box that tell about Anansi. Write those adjectives on the web. Add any other adjectives that tell about Anansi.

clever	funny	generous	foolish	shy
selfish	tricky	kind	strong	creative
impatient	loyal	lazy	brave	mischievous

Anansi
Learns to
Fish

All About Anansi

Read the sentences below that tell about the events in "Anansi Learns to Fish." Next, on the chart on page 141, fill in the setting and characters. Then, put the following events in the order in which they happened on the chart to summarize the story.

Turtle has Anansi set the net in the river.

Anansi wants to trick Turtle into catching a fish for Anansi to eat.

Anansi cooks the fish.

Anansi goes to the Justice Tree and tells his story.

Turtle has Anansi weave the net.

Anansi pulls in the net with a fish in it.

Anansi asks Turtle to show him how to catch fish, and Turtle agrees.

Turtle has Anansi gather vines to make a net.

Warthog rules in favor of Turtle.

Turtle eats the fish.

All About Anansi (page 2)

Anansi Learns to Fish

Setting

⬇

Characters

⬇

Events

⬇

⬇

⬇

⬇

⬇

⬇

⬇

⬇

It's a Trick!

Anansi sets out to trick Turtle but turns out to be the one who gets tricked. How did Turtle do it? Read the questions below. Your answers will tell how Turtle tricked Anansi. Write the answers from below in the Main Idea/Supporting Details chart on page 143.

1. What does Turtle say and do when it is time to gather the vines?

2. What does Turtle say and do when it is time to weave the net?

3. What does Turtle say and do when it is time to set the net?

4. What does Turtle say and do when it is time to cook the fish?

5. What does Turtle say and do when it is time to eat the fish?

Comprehension/Main Idea and Supporting Details   Listen, Read, and Learn With Classic Stories, Grade 3

Main Idea
Turtle tricks Anansi.

5   **Supporting Detail**

_____

_____

_____

4   **Supporting Detail**

_____

_____

_____

3   **Supporting Detail**

_____

_____

_____

2   **Supporting Detail**

_____

_____

_____

1   **Supporting Detail**

_____

_____

_____

Anansi
Learns to
Fish

Justice Rules

Whenever the jungle animals have disagreements, they take their troubles to Warthog at the Justice Tree. Help the animals by completing the following rules they should follow.

• Before you bring a disgreement to the Justice Tree, you must

first _____.

• If you come to the Justice Tree, each party must _____

_____.

• While Warthog is listening to both sides, it is important _____

_____.

• The parties must not _____

_____.

• Warthog will do his best to be _____.

• Once Warthog gives a decision, both parties must _____

_____.

Web of Words

Read each definition. Cut out the words at the bottom of the page. Match each word by gluing it to the space with its definition.

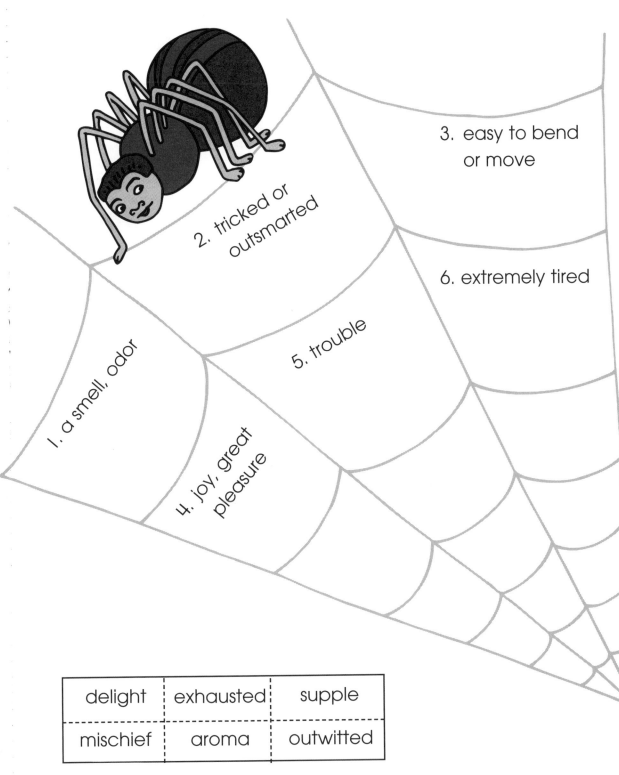

Anansi Learns to Fish

3. easy to bend or move

2. tricked or outsmarted

6. extremely tired

5. trouble

1. a smell, odor

4. joy, great pleasure

delight	exhausted	supple
mischief	aroma	outwitted

Fine Points

Read each question about the story. Answer in your own words.

Anansi
Learns to
Fish

1. At the beginning of the story, what does Anansi set out to do?

_____

2. Why does Anansi not want to get scratched?

_____

3. What does Turtle do each time while Anansi does the work?

_____

4. When does Anansi realize he's been tricked? _____

_____

5. What does Anansi do to get back at Turtle? _____

_____

6. What does Warthog say about Anansi's story? _____

_____

Collection of Words

Anansi
Learns to
Fish

At the beginning of the story, the author uses the words **big** and **huge** to describe Turtle's fish. These two words are synonyms. **Synonyms** are words that mean almost the same thing. Toward the end of the story, Anansi is **hungry** and Turtle is **full**. These two words are antonyms. **Antonyms** are words that mean the opposite of one another.

Think about synonyms and antonyms. Read the following clues, and write a word from the box.

friend	edge	scream
young	gather	together
simple	tired	tomorrow

1. Synonym for weary _____

2. Synonym for easy _____

3. Synonym for pal _____

4. Synonym for shriek _____

5. Antonym for middle _____

6. Antonym for scatter _____

7. Antonym for yesterday _____

8. Antonym for alone _____

Write one sentence using two antonyms.

_____

_____

Word Meaning/Synonyms and Antonyms   Listen, Read, and Learn With Classic Stories, Grade 3

Compare With Flair

In "Anansi Learns to Fish," Anansi thinks that fooling Turtle will be as simple as making a hyena laugh. The author uses the word **as** to compare two actions—fooling Turtle and making a hyena laugh. In other words, the spider thinks that his friend can be easily tricked. Any comparison that uses the word **as** or **like** is called a **simile** (SIHM uh lee).

Write a word or phrase from the box to complete each simile below.

honey	delicate white lace	an empty barrel	an arrow

1. The hungry spider felt as hollow as _____.

2. The fish moved through the water like _____.

3. The spider's web looked like _____.

4. The melon tasted as sweet as _____.

Now, try writing your own similes. Choose something to describe. Then, think of something that it can be compared with. Start with these phrases or use your own ideas.

The campfire was as bright as _____.

Those giraffes are as tall as _____.

The parrot sounded like _____.

About "Brer Rabbit and the Tar Baby"

Joel Chandler Harris knew what it was like to be hungry, lonely, and short of money. Born in 1848, he grew up never knowing his father. His mother worked as a seamstress to support herself and young Joel. When he was fourteen years old, he went to work for a newspaper publisher in order to improve his life and his mother's. While Harris was learning the trade, he lived on the publisher's plantation, where he used the owner's library to educate himself. Although Harris was white, during the lonely evenings, he enjoyed visiting African-American slaves who lived on the plantation. They told him wonderful stories that captured his imagination.

Years later, when Harris was a newspaperman working for the Atlanta Constitution, he remembered those evenings. He created Uncle Remus, an African-American character who told stories to a little white boy. When Harris printed the stories in the newspaper, they became very popular. He eventually retold more than 200 Uncle Remus stories, either in the newspaper or in books. "Brer Rabbit and the Tar Baby" is possibly the best-known of the stories.

Retold by Colleen Mulvenna

Brer Rabbit and the Tar Baby

Illustrated by Wendy Rasmussen

ne morning, Brer Fox got to thinking about all the trouble Brer Rabbit had been causing him. It seems Brer Rabbit always had a plan that meant trouble, did he. For instance, there was the ol' horse plan when Brer Rabbit persuaded Brer Fox that they could get a horse for free! Of course, Brer Fox, not wanting to miss anything free, became quite curious.

Brer Rabbit explained to Brer Fox that there was an old horse just lying on the ground over yonder. They could easily catch him and tie him up. Brer Fox considered Brer Rabbit's plan. Brer Fox quickly decided that this sounded like a great idea.

154

Brer Rabbit led Brer Fox over to the pasture. Sure enough, there was the horse lying on the ground just waiting to be caught. The trouble was that Brer Rabbit and Brer Fox couldn't decide how to get the job done.

After a while, Brer Rabbit came up with a plan, as he always did. "I'll tie you to the horse's tail," said Rabbit, said he. "When the horse tries to get up, you be sure to hold him down. I'd do it myself if I were as big and as strong as you are. I think this here's our plan—unless you're too scared to try."

There was something about the plan that made Brer Fox nervous, but he couldn't decide just what it was. Not wanting Brer Rabbit to think that he was a chicken, Brer Fox agreed to the plan.

And so Brer Rabbit tied Brer Fox to the horse's tail and exclaimed, "We got him, Brer Fox! I'm sure of it!"

Brer Fox smiled timidly, smiled he.

Brer Rabbit found himself a nice long stick and poked the horse on the backside—BAM! The horse jumped into midair and landed on his feet. Brer Fox, however, was upside down and swinging from that horse's tail.

When that horse felt something on his tail, he started jumping and bucking. Brer Fox suddenly realized what was wrong with Brer Rabbit's plan.

"Hold him tight, Brer Fox! Hold him tight!" Brer Rabbit yelled.

The horse jumped and turned and whinnied, but Brer Fox held on with all his might.

"Hold him tight, Brer Fox! Hold him tight!"

Brer Fox finally managed to shout, "I've got him, but who's gonna get ahold of me?"

Brer Rabbit simply repeated, "Hold him tight, Brer Fox! Hold him tight!"

Finally, Brer Fox got free and slid down the horse's tail, did he. But as he was on the way down, the horse kicked Brer Fox real hard. Brer Fox went higher and higher into the air. It was a week and four days before he came down again. This gave Brer Fox a whole lot of time to think about Brer Rabbit getting the best of him again.

Now, Brer Fox had finally thought of a way to give Brer Rabbit a taste of his own medicine.

First, Brer Fox mixed up a big batch of tar and shaped it into the form of a baby. When he finished making his Tar Baby, he put an old straw hat on her. Then, he sat her in the middle of the road. Brer Fox hid in the bushes and waited to see what might happen.

Well, just a short time later, who do you suppose came bouncing down the lane—lippity, loppity, lippity, loppity—as if he owned the world? It was none other than Brer Rabbit himself. Brer Fox stayed hidden in the bushes. As soon as Brer Rabbit saw the Tar Baby, he stopped dead in his tracks, stopped he.

"Good morning!" said Brer Rabbit, said he. "Beautiful day, isn't it?"

The Tar Baby didn't say a word, and Brer Fox stayed hidden in the bushes.

"How are you feeling today?" said Brer Rabbit, said he.

The Tar Baby didn't say a word, and Brer Fox almost started to chuckle.

"What's the matter with you? Can't you hear me?" said Brer Rabbit, said he. "If you can't, I can holler louder."

The Tar Baby was still quiet, and Brer Fox kept hidden.

"You're stuck-up," said Brer Rabbit, said he. "And I'm gonna cure you."

Brer Fox was having a hard time keeping quiet. But the Tar Baby didn't say a word.

Brer Rabbit hauled off and hit the Tar Baby right in the head. BOP! His fist stuck to the side of the Tar Baby's face. Brer Rabbit couldn't get loose.

"Let me go!" Brer Rabbit yelled. "Let me go, or I'll really let you have it!" And he smacked the Tar Baby on the other side of her head. BOP! Now his other fist was stuck.

Brer Rabbit was really mad now. "You turn me loose, or I'll make you sorry." THUNK! He kicked the Tar Baby, and his foot stuck fast. Brer Rabbit was hoppin' mad now, was he! He kicked the Tar Baby again with his other foot, and THUNK! Now that foot was stuck.

"You'd better let me loose, or I'm gonna butt you with my head." And Brer Rabbit butted the Tar Baby right under her chin. THUNK! Now his head stuck hard and fast to the silent Tar Baby.

Brer Fox strolled out from behind the bushes. He took one look at Brer Rabbit stuck to the Tar Baby. He laughed and laughed until he couldn't laugh anymore.

When Brer Fox picked himself up, he said, "Well, I think I finally got you this time, Brer Rabbit. You've been around here causing me trouble for too long a time, but now it's over."

"You're always putting your whiskers into something that's none of your business," said Brer Fox, said he. "Who invited you to strike up a conversation with this here Tar Baby? And who stuck you up the way you are? Nobody. You just stuck yourself to that Tar Baby without so much as an invitation. There you are, and there you'll stay until I get my fire and barbecue sauce ready."

For once in his life, Brer Rabbit was smart enough not to give any lip. In fact, he talked mighty humble. "Well, Brer Fox, you got me, and I bet there is no point in asking that you spare me."

"No, there isn't any point at all," Brer Fox agreed as he started gathering sticks for his fire.

"I guess today's the day that I'm going to be your dinner," Brer Rabbit said. "But getting barbecued is a whole lot better than being thrown into the briar patch." He sighed, sighed he. "That's for sure. Getting barbecued is almost a blessing compared to being thrown in the briar patch."

All this talk made Brer Fox stop and think. He sure enough wanted that rabbit to suffer. "Now that I think about it," said Brer Fox, "it's too hot to be standing over a hot fire. I think I'll string you up instead."

Brer Fox got to thinking again. "I can't string you up after all, Brer Rabbit—I didn't bring my rope. I guess I'll just have to throw you into that there pond."

Brer Rabbit began to sniffle, did he. "Please, Brer Fox. You know I can't stand to get my ears wet. But I guess being thrown into the pond, bad as it is, is still better than that there briar patch."

At last, Brer Fox was convinced that the worst thing he could do to Brer Rabbit was to toss him into the briar patch. With that, Brer Fox yanked Brer Rabbit right off the Tar Baby. Then, he tossed that rabbit right smack in the middle of the briar patch.

Brer Fox waited, but he didn't hear a sound. He waited and waited. Still not a sound came from the briar patch. Just when he was sure that he was rid of that nasty rabbit for good, he heard a little giggle.

"Tee-hee-hee! Tee-hee-hee!" Then the giggles broke into a roar of laughter.

Brer Fox looked up to see Brer Rabbit sitting comfortably on the top of the hill on the other side of the briar patch. Brer Fox had been tricked!

Brer Rabbit gave a smart-alecky wave. "I was born and raised in that there briar patch, Brer Fox! Born and raised in the briar patch! I know it like I know the back of my hand!" With that, Brer Rabbit hopped on over the hill and out of sight.

And that's when Brer Fox knew, knew it well did he, that he would never be rid of that trickster rabbit.

Bibliography
"Brer Rabbit and the Tar Baby"

Lester, Julius. *The Tales of Uncle Remus: The Adventures of Brer Rabbit*. Illustrated by Jerry Pinkney. New York: Puffin, 1999. With lively, contemporary language and humorous illustrations, this book includes the story of Brer Rabbit and the Tar Baby, and then some!

Parks, Van Dyke. *Jump on Over!: The Adventures of Brer Rabbit and His Family*. Illustrated by Barry Moser. San Diego: Harcourt Brace, 1989. This collection of somewhat less-familiar tales tells us again, with humor and brilliant illustrations, how Brer Rabbit uses his wit to keep himself and his family safe from the sharp teeth of enemies.

Kessler, Brad. *Brer Rabbit and Boss Lion*. Read by Danny Glover. New York: Simon & Schuster, 1996. Brer Rabbit must once again use his brain to overcome brawn. In this book, with accompanying audiocassette, he faces a hungry new neighbor, Boss Lion.

Johnston, Tony. *The Tale of Rabbit and Coyote*. Illustrated by Tomie dePaola. New York: Putnam, 1994. This folktale from Mexico is reminiscent of "Brer Rabbit and the Tar Baby." Rabbit eats the farmer's best chiles and gets stuck to a wax image the farmer has placed in the field. The farmer is so angry he prepares to make rabbit stew, but Rabbit manages to trick Coyote into changing places with him.

Stevens, Janet. *Tops and Bottoms*. San Diego: Harcourt Brace, 1995. This story inspired by folktales from various cultures features another trickster hare. Bear has money and land, but he is lazy. Hare has no wealth, but he has a hungry family and plenty of smarts. Hare makes a deal to work for Bear and—of course!—finds a way to outwit him.

Sticky Points—Details

Read each sentence. If the details were part of the story, write **yes**. If the details were not part of the story, write **no**.

1. Brer Fox tied himself to a bull's tail. _____

2. Brer Fox put a Tar Baby in the briar patch. _____

3. The Tar Baby said hello to Brer Rabbit, but it was really Brer Fox talking from the bushes. _____

4. Brer Rabbit ended up with his hands, feet, and head stuck to the Tar Baby. _____

5. Brer Fox asked his mother what he should do with Brer Rabbit. _____

6. Brer Fox said he wouldn't barbecue Brer Rabbit because he forgot how to make his sauce. _____

7. Brer Rabbit said that he'd rather get his ears wet in the pond than be thrown in the briar patch. _____

8. Brer Fox threw Brer Rabbit into the pond. _____

Brer Rabbit
and the
Tar Baby

Comprehension/Details

Listen, Read, and Learn With Classic Stories, Grade 3

Summing Up "Brer Rabbit"

Think about the story. Complete the summary chart to tell what the story was mostly about. Use the chart to tell someone who hasn't read "Brer Rabbit" about the story.

Brer Rabbit

Characters

Who is the story about?

_____

_____

Setting

Where does the story take place?

_____

_____

Summary

What are the main events that happen in the story?

_____

_____

_____

_____

_____

_____

Brer Rabbit
and the
Tar Baby

Briar Patch Match

Read the words on the left. Then, read the meanings on the right. Match each word to its meaning. Write the letter for the meaning in front of the word.

Brer Rabbit and the Tar Baby

1. _____ briar   A. a discussion

2. _____ chuckle   B. anxious or fearful

3. _____ pasture   C. to laugh quietly

4. _____ nervous   D. walked around in a slow, relaxed way

5. _____ curious   E. to shake from fear or cold

6. _____ strolled   F. talked into doing something

7. _____ timidly   G. a bush or vine with thorny stems

8. _____ tremble   H. in a shy way

9. _____ persuaded   I. eager to find out about something

10. _____ conversation J. ground where animals graze

Word Meaning/Story Vocabulary   Listen, Read, and Learn With Classic Stories, Grade 3

One Thing After Another

Cut out the sentence strips below. Use them to put the story events in order. Or glue each strip to a separate sheet of paper and illustrate it to make your own book.

"Let me go!" Brer Rabbit yelled. "Let me go, or I'll really let you have it."

- -

Brer Fox waited, but he didn't hear a sound.

- -

"There you are, and there you'll stay until I get my fire and barbecue sauce ready."

- -

When Brer Fox picked himself up, he said, "Well, I think I finally got you this time, Brer Rabbit."

- -

Brer Rabbit gave a smart-alecky wave.

- -

First, Brer Fox mixed up a big batch of tar and shaped it into the form of a baby.

- -

"Now that I think about it," said Brer Fox, "it's too hot to be standing over a hot fire. I think I'll string you up instead."

- -

"Good morning!" said Brer Rabbit, said he. "Beautiful day, isn't it?"

- -

Then, he tossed that rabbit right smack in the middle of the briar patch.

- -

"I didn't bring my rope. I guess I'll just have to throw you into that there pond."

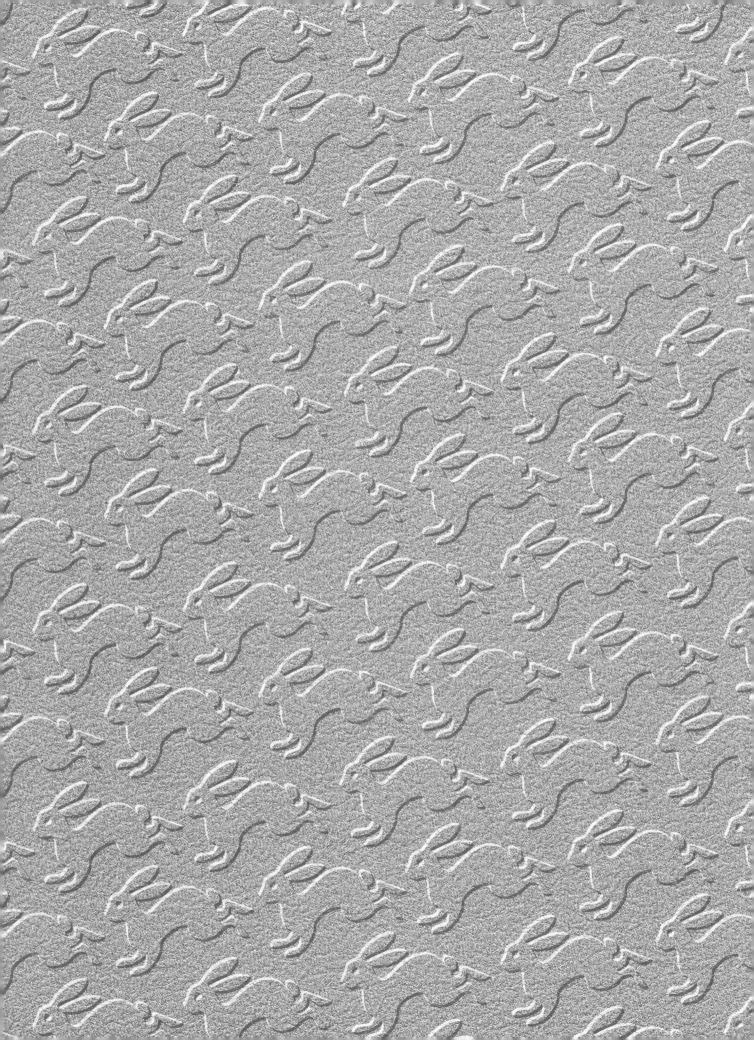

Why Did He Do It?

Why something happens is called the **cause**. The thing that happens is called the **effect**. Complete the chart to show cause and effect relationships from the story.

What Happens (Effect)	Why It Happens (Cause)
_____ _____	Brer Fox doesn't want Brer Rabbit to think he is a chicken.
Brer Rabbit gets angry when he tries to talk to the Tar Baby.	_____ _____
Brer Fox thinks he is getting the better of Brer Rabbit.	_____ _____
_____ _____	Brer Rabbit tricks Brer Fox into thinking that is the worst thing he can do to him.
At the end of the story, Brer Rabbit laughs at Brer Fox.	_____

Those Tricksters!

When you **compare** two or more things, you tell how they are alike. When you **contrast** them, you tell how they are different.

In what ways are Brer Rabbit and Brer Fox alike and different? Use the Venn diagram on the next page to compare and contrast the two characters. Read the phrases below. Decide if each phrase tells about only Brer Rabbit, only Brer Fox, or both Brer Rabbit and Brer Fox. Write each phrase in the correct place on the diagram.

always has a plan for everything

wants to eat the other one

falls for a trick

gets angry when someone won't talk to him

doesn't want the other one to think he is chicken

pulls a trick on the other one

Brer Rabbit
and the
Tar Baby

Comprehension/Compare and Contrast

Listen, Read, and Learn With Classic Stories, Grade 3

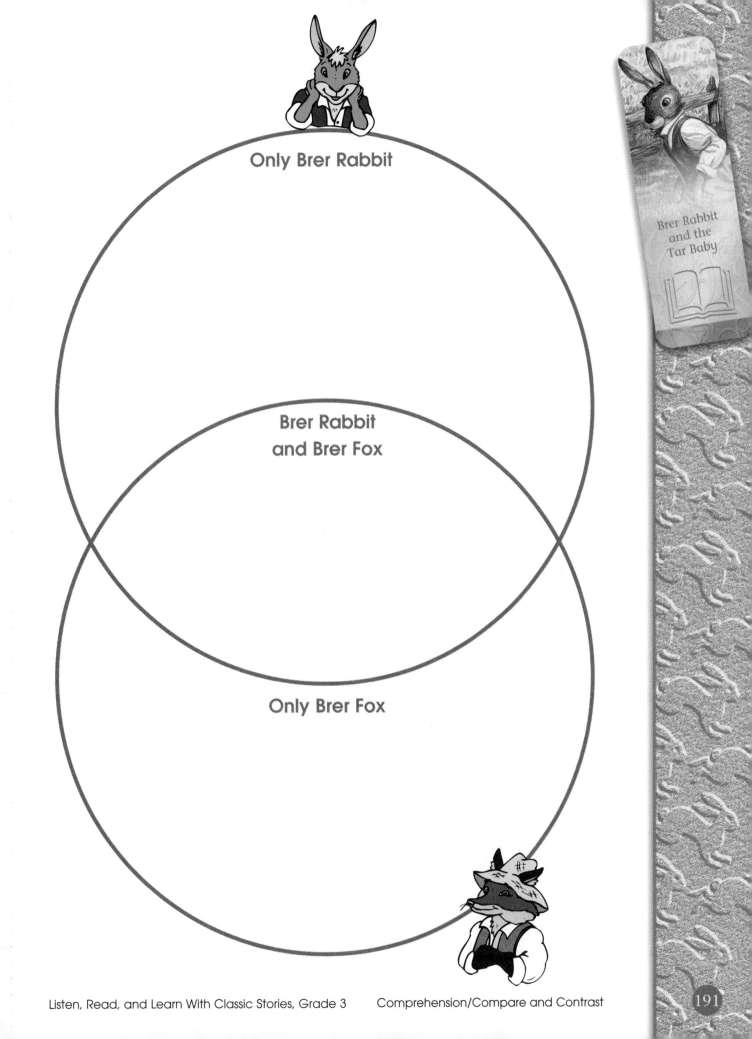

Only Brer Rabbit

Brer Rabbit
and Brer Fox

Only Brer Fox

What If?

The **point of view** of a story comes from the character telling the story. "Brer Rabbit and the Tar Baby" is told by someone who is not a character in the story. This is known as **third-person** point of view. The story is told using the pronouns **he**, **she**, and **they**. In a story told from the **first-person** point of view, the narrator (the person telling the story) is usually a character in the story. The narrator uses the pronouns **I** and **me** when talking about himself or herself, but can use the pronouns **he**, **she**, and **they** when talking about other characters in the story.

What if Brer Rabbit, Brer Fox, or even the Tar Baby told the story "Brer Rabbit and the Tar Baby"? Choose a part of the story. Rewrite it using the first-person point of view. If you need more space, continue on a separate sheet of paper.

"Here's the real story. . . ."

_____

_____

_____

_____

_____

_____

_____

_____

_____

Comprehension/Point of View   Listen, Read, and Learn With Classic Stories, Grade 3

Picture This

The illustrations for a story can give you clues about what is happening in the story. Look at the illustrations on the pages listed below. Then, answer each question.

1. **Page 153:** What is Brer Fox thinking about? _____

   _____

2. **Page 161:** How does the artist show that Brer Fox is high in the

   air? _____

   _____

3. **Page 162:** Using the illustration, how would you explain what a

   Tar Baby is to someone who has never seen one before?

   _____

   _____

4. **Page 164:** What do these three illustrations tell you about what

   is happening at this point in the story? _____

   _____

   _____

Brer Rabbit
and the
Tar Baby

Sounds Around

The **ou** sound can stand for more than one sound. Read the list of story words. Sort the words by writing each word in the correct column.

ground   shout   bouncing   around
sound   could   louder   would

ou as in **found**	**ou** as in **should**
_____	_____
_____	_____
_____	_____
_____	_____
_____	_____
_____	_____

Brer Rabbit and the Tar Baby

Hop on Opposites

Brer Rabbit told Brer Fox to hold on **tight** to the horse, but later he wanted the Tar Baby to turn him **loose**. **Antonyms** are words that have opposite meanings, such as **tight** and **loose**. Read the first word in each line. Then, draw a line to show how Brer Rabbit might hop from the first word to its opposite as in the example below.

tight	close	happy	strong	loose
1. **up**	high	down	near	above
2. **old**	new	far	worn	clean
3. **shout**	yell	whisper	ask	cry
4. **top**	middle	highest	bottom	even
5. **first**	leading	best	last	worst
6. **quiet**	careful	silent	calm	loud
7. **strong**	weak	brave	solid	firm
8. **wrong**	incorrect	bad	hurtful	right
9. **stop**	quit	end	begin	leave
10. **big**	large	small	huge	roomy

Brer Rabbit
and the
Tar Baby

Tell a Trickster Tale

Brer Rabbit plays tricks on Brer Fox. Write a trickster tale of your own below. If you need more space, continue on a separate sheet of paper.

Brer Rabbit and the Tar Baby

- **Set the scene.** Will the events take place at school? Under the ocean? On another planet?

- **Create characters.** Will they be people? Animals? Brer Rabbit? You? Will they have special powers? A good sense of humor?

- **At the beginning,** choose a point of view, and tell about the characters and the scene.

- **In the middle,** tell about the trick.

- **At the end,** explain if the trick succeeded or if the trickster was tricked instead.

A Note from Brer Rabbit

Read the note below and look for mistakes.
Find and correct three capitalization mistakes,
three punctuation mistakes, and two
spelling mistakes.

Dear brer Fox,

I think it is time we made up. would you like to visit me in the briar patch? I can't make your favorite barbecue, but I'll make som lemonade and cookies. Could you come this tuesday afternoon at 3 o'clock. Please let me no whether you can make it We can have such good times again. I promise that we won't go near any horses, and I won't even trick you one little bit? I can't wait to see you.

Your friend,

Brer Rabbit

About "John Henry: The Legend of a Steel-Driving Man"

The legend of John Henry most likely started in the work songs sung by laborers working on railroads in the South in the 1870s. There are many versions and hundreds of different recordings of the song. If John Henry was a real person, and John Henry was a very common name at that time, he was probably a former slave. Sometimes he is confused with an actual African-American man—John Hardy, a reported outlaw and the subject of other work songs.

The tunnel in the story was part of the Chesapeake and Ohio (C&O) Railroad. Most likely named for a bend in the nearby Greenbrier River, the Big Bend tunnel was built through the Allegheny Mountains between 1870 and 1873. (To find this bend on a map, look for the present-day city of Talcott.) At the time it was built, it was the longest tunnel in the United States—one and a quarter miles. The C&O Railroad is now part of the CSX System, a freight carrier whose primary cargo is coal. Many of its former railroads have now become hiking and biking trails.

The construction of the tunnels through the Allegheny Mountains required thousands of workers. The work was dangerous, and workers were often killed in dynamite explosions and rock falls. Although the steam drill was introduced in the South in the early 1870s, there is no record of a contest between the machine and any worker.

Regardless of the truth behind the legend, John Henry was highly regarded by African-American laborers in the South. To some people, his contest represents the conflict between people and machines. To others, it represents the challenges people face every day.

Retold by Susan M. Walker

John Henry: The Legend of a Steel-Driving Man

Illustrated by Steve Haefele

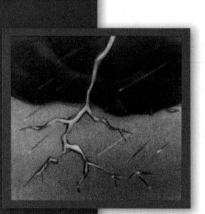

efore John Henry was born, a great thunderstorm shook the earth. Lightning flashed across the sky. His poor mama thought their little house would shake right off its base. But it didn't.

"I can feel it. This baby is not ordinary," said Mama.

"He's got a hammer in his hand!" said Papa.

John Henry grew faster than a weed in summer. By the time he was a year old, he could plow a field by himself. At age five, he could pick as much cotton as Mama and Papa combined.

What John Henry loved best, though, was hammering. He could hammer straighter and faster than anyone in the county.

One morning, John Henry said, "It's time for me to make my own way in the world."

"We'll miss you, John Henry," Papa sighed. "But we can't stand in your way."

"Take this," said Mama, holding out a brand new kerchief. "Wherever you go, it will remind you of us."

That day, John Henry was very busy. He helped a farmer clear huge trees from a new field. He built a house for the new schoolteacher, two barns for the Huckaby brothers, and a henhouse for Mrs. Wells. He even found Eliza's lost kitten.

John Henry traveled around the county doing all kinds of work. In return, the people he worked for gave him three meals a day and a place to sleep at night.

In spring, he helped farmers plow and plant their fields. In summer, he chopped the weeds that grew in the fields. In fall, he picked corn, potatoes, and cotton. In winter, he worked for a blacksmith fixing plows and other farm tools.

It was blacksmith work that John Henry liked best. As he pounded his hammer against the hot metal, he would sing quietly to himself.

"I was born with a hammer in my hand, oh yes. I was born with a hammer in my hand."

One spring evening, John Henry went for a walk. He saw a wagon stuck in the mud and offered to help. With one hand he dragged the wagon out of the mud.

That's when he saw Lucy Ann. Her dress was spattered with mud, but John Henry thought she was the prettiest woman he had ever seen.

That summer, John Henry went to work for the railroad. The boss put him to work hammering boulders into gravel. The gravel was needed to keep the track in place.

As John Henry worked, he sang quietly, "I was born with a hammer in my hand, oh yes. I was born with a hammer in my hand."

One day the boss called the men together.

"The work crew over by Big Bend has laid track as far as the mountains," he said. "But they need help getting through the mountains. They'll pay you twice as much as what you're getting paid here."

"Driving steel through solid rock is mighty hard work," the boss explained. "It's hotter and dustier than any work we've done here. That's what it takes to put a tunnel through solid rock."

"You can count on me," said John Henry, "for I was born with a hammer in my hand, oh yes. I was born with a hammer in my hand."

That evening, John Henry went to tell Lucy Ann about the Big Bend tunnel.

"It's calling out to me, Lucy Ann," he said. "I've got to go."

"Well, then," said Lucy Ann, "if you've got to go, then I'll go, too. I've got family in that part of the country, and I know they could use my help."

When they got to Big Bend, John Henry followed the train tracks until he came to the work crew. "I've come from Monroe County, and I'm here to drive steel."

"Just a minute, mister," said the boss. "To drive steel, you've got to hammer straight, and you've got to be as strong as an ox."

"I can do it," said John Henry. "Which one of you shakers will hold the spike for me?"

At once, every man on the work crew stared down at his feet. Finally, Little Bill stepped forward, picked up a spike, and put it in place.

Before anyone could blink, WHOOSH went the hammer, and RING went the spike. With one stroke, the spike went clear into the rock.

"You're hired!" said the boss as the work crew cheered.

All summer the crew hammered away at the mountain, making slow but steady progress. Some days the sun was so hot and the air was so still that the crew worked at a snail's pace. That is, everyone except John Henry. He drove twice as much steel to make up for the rest of the crew.

A salesman appeared one day to challenge the work crew. "This machine, my steam drill, can drill faster than any man, and I can prove it," he told the boss. "Let's have a contest. If the machine wins, you'll buy it. If the man wins, I'll give you the drill."

"Wait," John Henry interrupted. "If I win, the men get to keep working until they finish the tunnel."

After a moment, the boss agreed.

After supper, John Henry walked to Lucy Ann's house to tell her about the contest.

"They're counting on me," he said. "I don't want to let the crew down."

"You can do it, John Henry," said Lucy Ann. "You were born with a hammer in your hand, oh yes. You were born with a hammer in your hand."

The day of the contest was the hottest day all summer. There wasn't even the slightest hint of a breeze.

John Henry and Little Bill got set. The salesman rolled the steam drill into position. He began pushing levers and pulling knobs. The machine sputtered and coughed. Finally, wisps of black smoke rose from its smokestack.

"Let the contest begin!" shouted the boss.

W HOOSH! RING! went John Henry's hammer against the steel spike.

RAT-TAT-TAT-TAT! pounded the steam drill against the rock.

"Come on, John Henry!" roared the growing crowd.

"The steam drill is ahead!" shouted one man.

"No! John Henry is ahead!" shouted another man.

At the end of the first hour, sweat poured off John Henry. The steam drill chugged along, while the black smoke got a little bit thicker.

"How are we doing, Little Bill?" asked John Henry.

"The machine's ahead," said Little Bill.

"We'll catch it," said John Henry.

WHOOSH! RING!

RAT-TAT-TAT-TAT!

At the end of the second hour, the crowd could see that the steam drill was ahead. The work crew and the boss were getting worried.

"John Henry is the best steel driver there is," said Lucy Ann. "He's not going to lose to that machine."

At the end of the third hour, Little Bill said, "John Henry, the machine is winning. You've got to do something."

John Henry thought as he pounded. Then he spoke. "This ten-pound hammer is too small. Hand me that twenty-pound hammer."

At the end of the fourth hour, John Henry had gained on the steam drill, but he was still behind.

WHOOSH, RING!

RAT-TAT-TAT-TAT!

"I can't let the crew down," John Henry said. "Hand me another twenty-pound hammer, Little Bill."

WHOOSH, RING! WHOOSH, RING! went John Henry's two hammers.

"Look at him go!" shouted a man in the crowd. "I never saw a man do that."

"John Henry is no ordinary man," said Lucy Ann.

At the end of the fifth hour, the sun was straight overhead. There was still no sign of a breeze. Every person in the crowd had found a spot in the shade. Some people even dozed off, but John Henry and the steam drill kept going.

At the end of the sixth hour, John Henry was
tired, and he knew that the steam drill was still
ahead. He thought about how much the work crew
needed their jobs. He thought about how much Lucy
Ann believed in him.

John Henry began to hammer faster and faster. The
amazed crowd stood up and began to cheer.

WHOOSH, RING! WHOOSH, RING!

"John Henry's ahead!" cried a boy.

John Henry couldn't hear the crowd's cheers or the
RAT-TAT-TAT-TAT of the steam drill. All he could
hear was a familiar song playing faintly in his head.
"I was born with a hammer in my hand, oh yes. I
was born with a hammer in my hand."

Suddenly, black smoke poured from the steam drill as it sputtered to a stop. The salesman pulled and pushed and tugged and pounded, but the machine wouldn't start.

WHOOSH, RING! WHOOSH, RING! John Henry had the lead! The crowd was cheering wildly, but John Henry couldn't hear them.

The salesman worked on the steam drill for almost an hour. John Henry kept up the pace and increased his lead by several feet. Finally, the steam drill sputtered and hissed and started up again. But it was clear to all how the contest would end.

"Time's up!" shouted the boss.

John Henry sunk to the ground while a man on the work crew made the measurements.

"The steam drill has gone nine feet into the mountain," said the man, "but John Henry has gone fifteen feet."

These were the last words that John Henry ever heard. He had hammered so hard and so fast that his heart burst right then and there. But he died doing what he loved best—hammering and blacksmithing.

John Henry was buried on a hill overlooking the tunnel he helped build. To this day, whenever a train goes through the tunnel, you can hear the wind sing:

I was born with a hammer in my hand, oh yes.
I was born with a hammer in my hand.

Is This Story True?

Probably not, but the story is based on truth. A former slave named John Henry probably lived in West Virginia in the 1870s. The tunnel is also real. It was built in West Virginia. At the time, the tunnel was the longest one in the world. There's no record of the contest, but the steam drill was used in the South around that time.

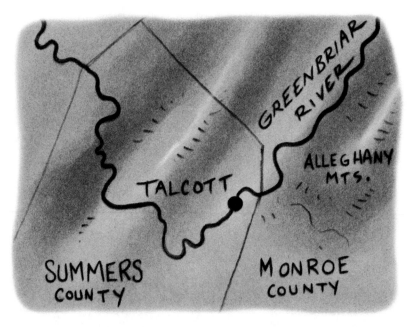

Bibliography
"John Henry: The Legend of a Steel-Driving Man"

Keats, Ezra Jack. *John Henry: An American Legend*. New York: Knopf, 1987. The award-winning author/illustrator presents the story of John Henry beautifully, with rhythmic text and powerful illustrations.

Lester, Julius. *John Henry*. Illustrated by Jerry Pinkney. New York: Dial, 1994. This Caldecott Honor Book is a vigorous retelling of the old ballad of John Henry. It has been called a "celebration of the human spirit."

San Souci, Rober D. *Larger Than Life: The Adventures of American Legendary Heroes*. New York: Doubleday, 1991. This book includes five dynamic stories of legendary American figures: John Henry, Old Stormalong, Slue-Foot Sue and Pecos Bill, Strap Buckner, and Paul Bunyan.

Kellogg, Steven. *Pecos Bill: A Tall Tale*. New York: Morrow, 1986. This tall tale is about the larger-than-life hero named Pecos Bill, who—so the story goes—was raised by a coyote in the Texas wilderness and grew up to become the first cattle rancher.

Thomassie, Tynia. *Feliciana Feydra LeRoux: A Cajun Tall Tale*. Illustrated by Cat Bowman Smith. Boston: Little Brown, 1995. Feliciana's grandfather refuses to take her alligator hunting, so she sneaks out to the swamp to follow Grandpa and her brothers. Feliciana turns out to be more than a match for an alligator.

Order in the Chart

Read the events. Write them in the chart to show the order in which they happened in the story.

A salesman challenged the work crew.

John Henry left home to make his own way.

John Henry was born with a hammer in his hand.

John Henry died.

John Henry won the contest against the steam drill.

John Henry went to work building the railroad.

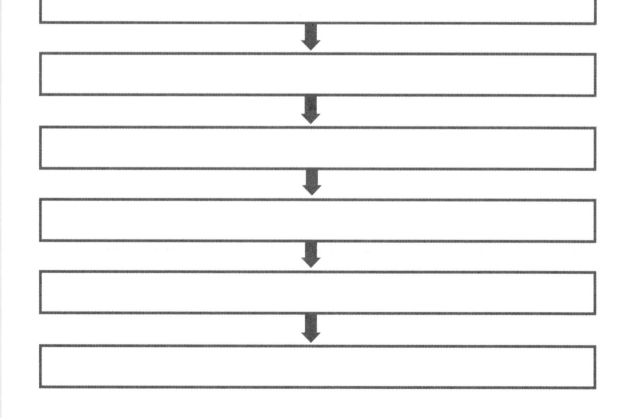

Comprehension/Sequencing   Listen, Read, and Learn With Classic Stories, Grade 3

Add It Up to a Story

Answer the following questions about the important parts of the story "John Henry."

1. Who is the main character in this story?

   _____

2. Name at least two other characters in the story.

   _____

3. Where does most of the action in the story happen?

   _____

4. Think of one object in the story to remind people of John Henry. Tell what object you chose and why you think it was important to John Henry.

   _____

   _____

5. Sum up the story. In a few sentences, tell the main things that happened in the story.

   _____

   _____

   _____

   _____

John Henry:
The Legend
of a Steel-
Driving Man

The Big Idea

Reread page 198. Read the statements in the Main Idea box below. Write the main idea in the chart. Read the statements in the Supporting Details box. Write the details that support the main idea.

John Henry: The Legend of a Steel-Driving Man

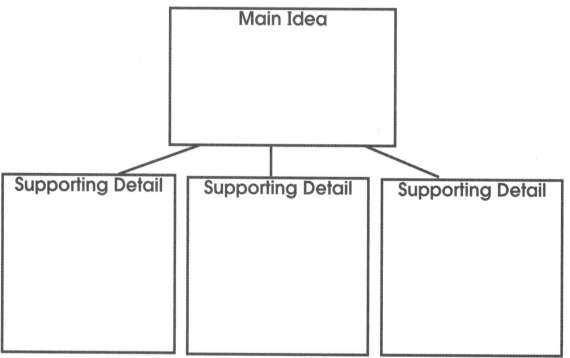

Main Idea

Supporting Detail	Supporting Detail	Supporting Detail

Main Idea

- John Henry left home to travel the world.
- The hero John Henry is sometimes confused with an outlaw.
- The legend of John Henry is based on real events.

Supporting Details

- Many parts of the old railroads are now hike and bike trails.
- The building of the railroads required thousands of workers.
- The tunnel was part of the C&O Railroad.
- John Henry was not an ordinary man.
- The steam drill was introduced in the South in the 1870s.
- The story was popular in the South.

Hammering Out the Details

Cut out the hammers at the bottom of the page. Read each sentence. If the sentence tells something that happened in the story, glue a hammer in the box. Some hammers may be left over.

1. When John Henry left home, his mother gave him a book.

2. John Henry first saw Lucy Ann when he was getting a wagon out of the mud.

3. When John Henry was showing the boss he could drive steel, Little Bill held the spike for him.

4. John Henry didn't drive as much steel as the rest of the railroad crew.

5. In the contest, John Henry used two hammers at one time.

6. John Henry was in first place throughout the whole contest.

7. During the contest, the steam drill sputtered to a stop.

8. John Henry wanted to win the contest so the men could keep working.

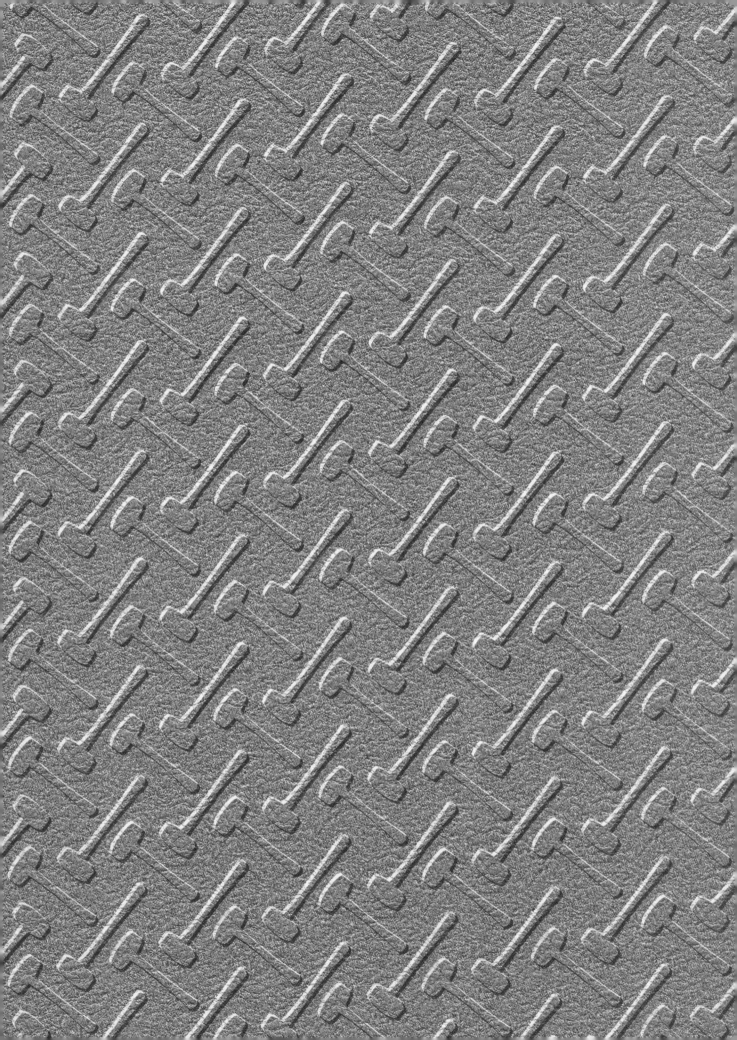

A Hero's Story

A **legend** tells the story of a hero from the past. When the story is first told, it may be factual. As it is told again and again, parts of it grow larger than truth. This is called **exaggeration**.

John Henry: The Legend of a Steel-Driving Man

Examples:

Events from the story that could really happen have pink squares. Exaggerated story events have blue squares.

- born during a thunderstorm

- learned to pick cotton when he was a little boy

- born with a hammer in his hand

- at age five, could pick as much cotton as two adults

Read the story events below. Choose your two favorite colors or patterns to complete the key. Then, use the key to color the squares.

Key	
☐	☐
could really happen	exaggeration

- ☐ pulled a wagon out of the mud with one hand

- ☐ got a red kerchief from his mother

- ☐ helped a little girl find her kitten

- ☐ built a house, two barns, and a henhouse in one day

- ☐ worked for the railroad as a steel driver

- ☐ worked hard in hot weather

The Steel-Driving Man

John Henry: The Legend of a Steel-Driving Man

Think about the character John Henry. Circle words in the following lists that describe him.

unique

popular

forgetful

driven

unkind

cranky

brave

determined

dishonest

helpful

dependable

ordinary

shy

hard worker

loyal

independent

foolish

imaginative

Comprehension/Characterization   Listen, Read, and Learn With Classic Stories, Grade 3

The Steel-Driving Man (page 2)

Read these events from the story. Think about what they tell about John Henry. Match each example with a character trait from the previous page.

1. _____ John Henry decides it is time for him to make his own way in the world.

2. _____ John Henry helps someone pull a wagon from the mud.

3. _____ John Henry does twice the work of the rest of the crew.

4. _____ The crowd cheers wildly for John Henry.

5. _____ John Henry can do things no ordinary man can do.

Choose a character trait from the previous page that is not included in the examples above. Write the trait and an example from the story that explains why you think John Henry has that trait.

6. _____

_____

_____

_____

Joined Together

Compound words are two words that are joined together to make a new word. Draw lines to match pairs of words to form compounds from the story. Write the new words on the lines.

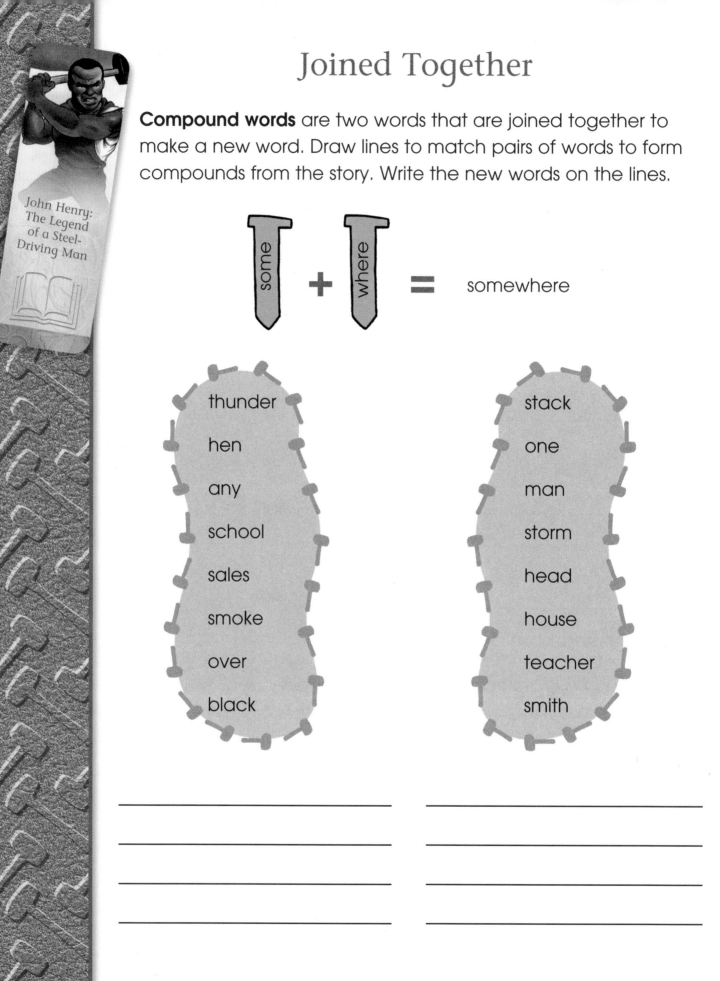

some + where = somewhere

thunder	stack
hen	one
any	man
school	storm
sales	head
smoke	house
over	teacher
black	smith

_____   _____

_____   _____

_____   _____

_____   _____

Word Structure/Compound Words   Listen, Read, and Learn With Classic Stories, Grade 3

John Henry:
The Legend
of a Steel-
Driving Man

Story Word-Stock

Read the definition on each car. In the blank, write the word from the list that matches the meaning.

John Henry: The Legend of a Steel-Driving Man

a large rock
_____

fell into a light sleep
_____

regular, common
_____

ordinary   challenge

spattered   dozed

faintly   wisps

boulder

splashed, speckled
_____

thin lines or little bits
_____

slightly, barely
_____

dare, invite to compete
_____

Take a Like Hike

John Henry: The Legend of a Steel-Driving Man

Writers often use comparisons to make their stories more interesting. One type of comparison is called a **simile** (SIHM-uh-lee). A simile uses the words **like** or **as** to compare two things.

Examples:

John Henry was **like** a barn.

He was **as** tall **as** a tree.

Hike along the Greenbriar River. Complete the similes with words from the box. You will not use all the words.

a machine	a picture	fire	fish
an ox	a mountain	a weed	a family
snails	lightning	an owl	bees

John Henry didn't work like a man, but more like _____.

John Henry was as strong as _____.

John Henry grew faster than _____.

Grammar/Similes

Listen, Read, and Learn With Classic Stories, Grade 3

The crew was as busy as _____.

John Henry was built like _____.

The sun was as hot as _____.

The heat made the crew move as slowly as _____.

John Henry thought Lucy Ann was as pretty as _____.

Grammar/Similes

243

An Eyewitness Account

Pretend you are someone who watched the contest between John Henry and the steam drill. Complete each sentence.

That day of the contest between John Henry and the steam drill

was _____.

It all started when _____

_____

_____

_____.

I watched as John Henry _____

_____

_____

_____.

I couldn't believe it when _____

_____

_____

_____.

The most exciting moment was _____

_____

_____

_____.

I'll never forget that day because _____

_____

_____.

John Henry: The Legend of a Steel-Driving Man

Creative Writing/A Description

Listen, Read, and Learn With Classic Stories, Grade 3

Sign Up

Read the following poster advertising the contest between John Henry and the steam drill. Find and correct three capitalization mistakes, three punctuation mistakes, and two spelling mistakes. Make your corrections above each mistake or within the paragraph.

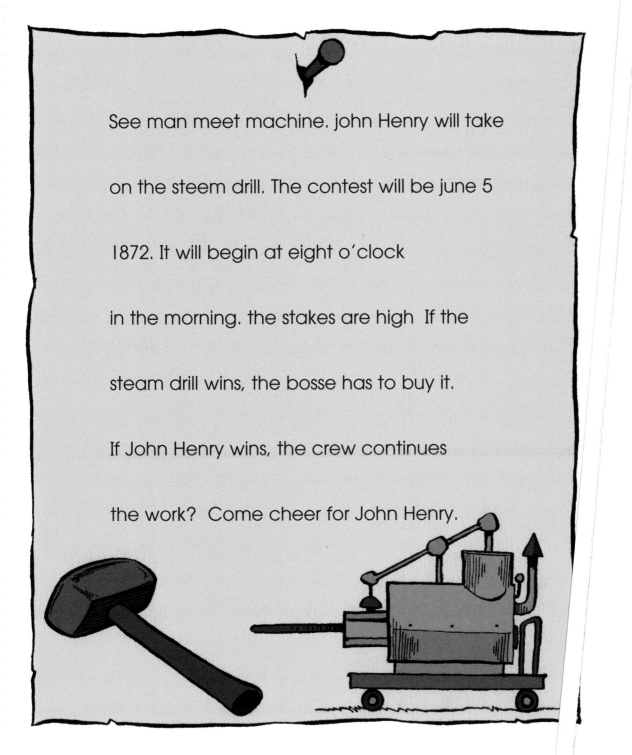

John Henry: The Legend of a Steel-Driving Man

See man meet machine. john Henry will take

on the steem drill. The contest will be june 5

1872. It will begin at eight o'clock

in the morning. the stakes are high If the

steam drill wins, the bosse has to buy it.

If John Henry wins, the crew continues

the work? Come cheer for John Henry.

About "Ali Baba and the Forty Thieves"

"Ali Baba and the Forty Thieves" is part of a collection of tales known as *1001 Arabian Nights*. Other well-known characters in the tales are Sinbad the Sailor and Aladdin. The history of this collection is a bit mysterious, as are the tales themselves. It is not known exactly where they were first told, or who told them, but they are certain to have been of Middle Eastern and Far Eastern origin, mostly from Arabia (now the countries in the Arabian Peninsula), Persia (modern-day Iran), India, and China.

The heroine of the tales is the legendary Scheherazade (sheh-hair-uh-ZAHD). The ruler of her country, the sultan, had a wife who betrayed him. He then vowed to take a new wife each night and have her put to death in the morning. Eventually, he married Scheherazade, but the clever young woman had a plan. On the wedding night, she told a delightful tale and stopped at the most interesting part, leaving the sultan in suspense. To hear the end of the tale, the sultan decided to let her live one more day. The next day, Scheherazade finished her story and began another. Again, the sultan let her live so he could hear the end. Scheherazade kept up this scheme for a thousand and one nights. During this time, she proved to the sultan that she could be a wise and devoted wife. They lived happily together for the rest of their lives. The story of Scheherazade is believed to be make-believe, simply a way to connect the many different stories together.

For centuries, the tales were handed down by word of mouth. The first published volume was a French translation in the early 1700s. Since then, the tales have been translated into other languages and enjoyed by readers around the world.

Retold by Melissa Blackwell Burke

Ali Baba and the Forty Thieves

Illustrated by Holly Hannon

ong ago and far away in Persia, there lived two brothers named Cassim and Ali Baba. Cassim married a rich woman and became a wealthy merchant. While Cassim enjoyed a life of plenty, Ali Baba struggled. He provided for his wife and family by cutting wood and selling it in the marketplace.

One day, as Ali Baba worked in the forest, a troop of evil-looking men rode toward him. He thought that they might be a band of robbers, so Ali Baba scrambled up a tree to hide.

Ali Baba watched from above as the men on horseback stopped just under the tree. As the men tied up their horses, Ali Baba counted forty of them.

The captain of the troop stepped in front of a huge rock. "Open, Sesame!" he called.

At this, the rock rolled back and revealed a cave. The captain sent in the forty thieves, each carrying a full saddlebag. The captain followed the last man in and called, "Close, Sesame!" The rock rolled back over the opening, and everything fell silent.

Ali Baba waited patiently, for if he climbed down and they caught him, it would mean his doom. After a time, the rock slid open once more. The captain led as the forty thieves filed out of the cave. Their saddlebags now lay flat and empty.

When the last man was out, the captain called, "Close, Sesame!" The cave closed, and the band returned the way they had come.

Ali Baba slid down the tree. He simply had to try the magic words. He walked to the very spot where the captain had stood. "Open, Sesame!" he called.

Just as before, the great rock slid back. Ali Baba stepped into the cave, prepared for it to be dark. To Ali Baba's surprise, the cave was brightly lit by an opening at the top.

As Ali Baba looked around, he was amazed by what he saw. Gold and silver coins lay in great heaps. Beautiful rugs and expensive silk cloth were rolled and stacked one upon the other. Everywhere he looked, he saw piles of riches.

Ali Baba thought about what lay before him. He decided that with all this wealth, the robbers would not miss a few bags of gold. Quickly, he filled some sacks with gold coins and slipped out of the cave.

"Close, Sesame!" he commanded.

Ali Baba then led his donkey home.

Ali Baba told his wife all that had happened as he poured the coins from the bag.

"We must keep this a secret," Ali Baba said. "I will bury the gold. We will use a bit at a time, and no one will suspect our treasure."

"Let me measure the gold first," begged his wife. "Dig the hole, while I borrow a weighing pan."

Ali Baba's wife went to Cassim's house and asked to borrow a scale. Cassim's wife was curious about what her husband's poor brother would need to measure. Without saying a word, Cassim's wife put some honey on the bottom of the pan.

The trick worked. When Ali Baba returned the scale, a piece of gold was stuck to the bottom.

That evening, Cassim's wife informed her husband of his brother's new wealth.

"Ali Baba is so rich," she said, "that he doesn't count his gold. He weighs it." She showed him the gold coin stuck on the bottom of the scale.

Cassim rushed to Ali Baba's house and demanded to know about the gold. Ali Baba confessed his secret.

Cassim was overcome with greed. The next morning, he packed all ten of his donkeys and went in search of the cave. He found it soon enough, and he, too, cried, "Open, Sesame!"

Cassim entered the cave and remembered to call, "Close, Sesame." For a moment, he just stood and marveled at the wealth around him. Then, he began to stuff treasure after treasure into his bags.

When Cassim realized he could carry no more, he moved to leave the cave. He stood at the rock, but he could not remember the magic words.

"Open, Barley!" he cried, but the door wouldn't budge. Cassim tried many other words, but not the right one.

Soon, the forty thieves returned. When they saw Cassim's donkeys, the robbers realized someone was inside their cave. They rushed in with swords drawn and put an end to Cassim.

As night drew near without Cassim's return, his wife became uneasy. She sent for Ali Baba, who set out at once in search of his brother. At the cave, Ali Baba was quick to find Cassim. Sadly, Ali Baba wrapped him in silk and took him home.

Ali Baba told his servant Morgiana of the happenings and asked for her help. Morgiana was a clever woman. Ali Baba knew he could count on her to help make Cassim's wife understand the importance of keeping the cave a secret. Otherwise, the thieves would discover that others knew about the cave. Then, the thieves would surely come for them as well.

The next day, the thieves returned
to the cave and were shocked to find
Cassim's body gone. The captain
said, "Someone took it. Not one, but
two must have known our secret. We
must find the one who knows. If not,
we will lose everything."

The captain continued, "One of
you must go to the village. Find the
one who knows too much!"

One thief disguised himself and walked through the market. He heard merchants talking of Cassim's death and spoke to them.

"I have traveled here to see my old friend Cassim," he said. "I hear he has died. I must pay my respects to his family. Will you please show me his brother's home?"

The merchant pointed out the home. The thief later marked it with a chalk sign so he could recognize it again quickly. Then, the thief returned to the cave to report to the captain.

When Morgiana left the house that day, she noticed the mark. She was afraid it might be connected to Cassim's death and the thieves. She got a piece of chalk and marked all the other houses nearby. Ali Baba's house no longer stood out.

Later, the captain and the thieves went into the village. The one thief tried to lead the others to the house he had marked. But when so many other houses were marked as well, he grew confused.

"So which one is it?" the angry captain demanded. The frightened thief could not remember.

The captain paid a villager to point out Cassim's brother's house. The captain stared at the house, so he could not forget it.

The captain then dressed as an oil merchant. On his cart were many oil jars, but only one was filled with oil. An armed thief was stuffed into each of the other jars. He made his way to Ali Baba's house.

Ali Baba rested outside in the coolness of the evening. As the disguised captain passed by, he stopped and spoke to Ali Baba. "I have traveled some distance to sell this oil at market tomorrow," he said. "Tonight I find myself tired with no place to rest. May I stay here for the night?"

As was the custom, Ali Baba welcomed the man into his home.

Before the captain left the cart, he whispered into each jar, "At the signal, be ready to attack."

Morgiana helped get the guest settled. As she moved on to other work, her lamp went out. There was no more oil in the house. She remembered the oil outside in the merchant's jars. She would use a bit, and tell the merchant in the morning.

When she started to open a jar, a deep voice from inside asked, "Is it time?"

Most would have screamed in fear, but not Morgiana. "Not yet, but soon," she whispered.

Morgiana stopped at each jar, each time giving the same answer. She realized the danger and came up with a plan.

Morgiana led the donkey cart full of thieves to a high hill outside the village. One by one, she rolled the jars from the cart. The thieves inside were so frightened that they were never heard from again.

When the captain went to signal his men, they had disappeared. Alarmed, the captain quickly rode back to the cave.

In the morning, Morgiana told all to Ali Baba. The two knew then that the oil merchant and his men were really the captain and the thieves. Ali Baba realized that Morgiana had surely saved all of their lives.

But the captain had another plan. He disguised himself as an elderly merchant in the village. Each day, he spoke with Ali Baba. Ali Baba invited his new friend to have dinner in his home.

When the guest arrived, Morgiana grew uneasy. As he reached for a dish, Morgiana saw a dagger hidden in the man's clothing. She then recognized the guest as the captain of the thieves.

Again, Morgiana thought quickly. She put on a costume and began to dance in front of Ali Baba and the captain. Suddenly, Morgiana pulled out a dagger from under her costume. She drove the captain from their home and from their lives forever.

"What have you done?" Ali Baba shouted.

Morgiana answered, "I have saved us. You were entertaining the enemy, the captain of the thieves."

Ali Baba knew that the captain would have done him harm. He was so grateful to Morgiana that he asked her if she wanted to marry his son. When the two of them agreed, they were wed.

Ali Baba told his son the secret of the cave, who in time told his own son. Ali Baba and his family were rich for all of their days.

Bibliography
"Ali Baba and the Forty Thieves"

McVitty, Walter. *Ali Baba and the Forty Thieves*. New York: Abrams, 1989. Retold and illustrated by Walter McVitty, this delightful tale of Ali Baba is illustrated in the style of ancient Persian miniatures.

Kimmel, Eric A. *The Tale of Ali Baba and the Forty Thieves: A Story from the Arabian Nights*. New York: Holiday House, 1996. This retelling is lively and exciting, told with Kimmel's usual wit.

Kimmel, Eric A. *The Tale of Aladdin and the Wonderful Lamp: A Story from the Arabian Nights*. New York: Holiday House, 1992. Probably the two most-familiar tales of the 1001 Arabian Nights are the stories of Ali Baba and Aladdin. This delightful retelling is about Aladdin, the clever boy who defeats an evil sorcerer with the help of a magic lamp and a powerful genie.

Kimmel, Eric A. *The Three Princes: A Tale from the Middle East*. Illustrated by Leonard Everett Fisher. New York: Holiday House, 1994. Prince Fahad, Prince Muhammed, and Prince Moshen all want to marry the same beautiful and wise princess. She must decide by putting all three to a test.

Shepard, Aaron. *Forty Fortunes: A Tale of Iran*. New York: Clarion Books, 1999. When the royal treasure is stolen, the king hires Ahmed to find it. Ahmed fears the punishment that surely awaits him if he does not find the treasure within forty days.

Dare to Compare the Brothers

Read each phrase below. Decide if it describes Ali Baba or Cassim. Write the phrase in the space under the correct picture.

- can't keep a secret from his brother
- has help from a clever servant
- dies at the hands of the thieves
- shares the secret with his son

- wealthy merchant
- humble woodcutter
- overcome with greed
- forgets magic words

Ali Baba and the Forty Thieves

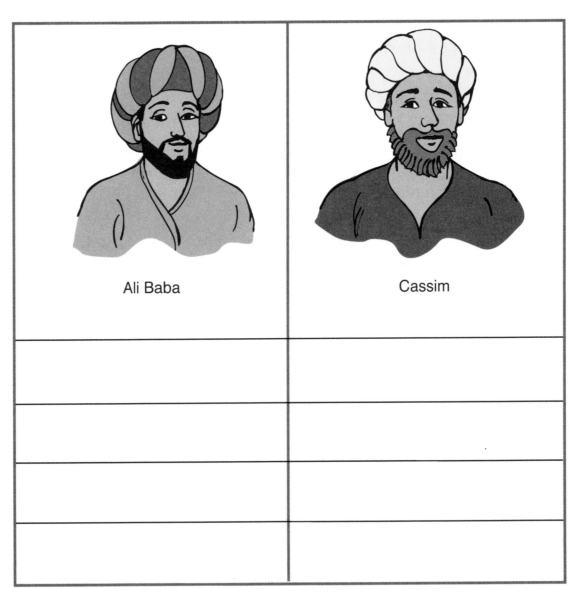

Ali Baba	Cassim

Comprehension/Analyze Characters   Listen, Read, and Learn With Classic Stories, Grade 3

Sum of the Parts

Complete the chart below to tell about the different parts of the story "Ali Baba and the Forty Thieves."

Ali Baba and the Forty Thieves

Setting

_____

_____

_____

Main Characters

_____

_____

_____

Summary

_____

_____

_____

_____

_____

_____

Ali Baba
and the
Forty Thieves

A Solution for Every Problem

Read and answer each question about
how Morgiana solves problems in the story.

Ali Baba
and the
Forty Thieves

1. What did Morgiana do after the thieves marked Ali Baba's
   house with chalk to help them find it again later?

   _____

   _____

   _____

2. What did Morgiana do when a thief asked from inside the oil
   jar, "Is it time yet?" Why?

   _____

   _____

   _____

3. Why did Morgiana roll the oil jars with the thieves in them
   down the hill?

   _____

   _____

   _____

4. What did Morgiana do at the end of the story that saved
   Ali Baba's life?

   _____

   _____

   _____

Which Came First?

Cut out the sentence strips below. Use them to put the story events in order. Or glue each to the top of a half sheet of construction paper, and illustrate each page. Staple the pages together to make your own book.

Ali Baba
and the
Forty Thieves

Cassim says, "Open, Barley!"

Ali Baba goes to the forest to cut wood.

Morgiana figures out that their dinner guest is really the evil captain of the thieves.

Ali Baba cannot believe his eyes when he sees what is inside the cave.

Ali Baba and his family live a safe and rich life.

Morgiana puts chalk marks on other houses.

The captain drives up to Ali Baba's house in a cart filled with oil jars.

Morgiana rolls all the jars down a hill.

The captain is driven away forever.

Who Said That?

Read each sentence. Think about which character from the story might have spoken the words. Write the character's name to complete the sentence.

ALI BABA   CASSIM   MORGIANA   THE CAPTAIN

1. "One of you must go to the village. Find the one who knows too much," said _____ .

2. "I have saved us. You were entertaining the enemy," said

_____ .

3. "If we use a little bit of gold at a time, no one will suspect our treasure," said _____ .

4. "I demand to know what you measured with my scale!" said _____ .

5. "Open, Barley!" shouted _____ .

6. "I'll put a chalk mark on all the other houses to make them look the same," said _____ .

7. "At the signal, be ready to leap from your jars and attack," said _____ .

Ali Baba
and the
Forty Thieves

Clues to a Conclusion

Answer the following questions by drawing conclusions.

1. When the thieves first go into the cave, their saddlebags are full. When they come out, they are empty. Why?

_____

_____

2. As Ali Baba watches the thieves, he makes sure he stays well hidden. Why?

_____

_____

3. When Cassim's body is gone the next day, the thieves figure something out. What?

_____

_____

4. Ali Baba says that Cassim's wife must be kept quiet about the way Cassim died. Why?

_____

_____

5. When Ali Baba realizes that Morgiana saved their lives, he asks if she wants to marry his son. Why?

_____

_____

Comprehension/Drawing Conclusions   Listen, Read, and Learn With Classic Stories, Grade 3

Long Ago and Far Away in Persia

The **setting** of a story is the time and place in which a story happens. Think about the setting of "Ali Baba and the Forty Thieves." Read the list of places and things below. Circle the ones that belong in the setting for this story. Draw a line through those that don't belong.

Ali Baba and the Forty Thieves

telephone

saddlebags

gold coins

city park

marketplace

oil jar

cave

computer

dagger

beautiful rugs

weighing pan

swords

village

bus station

silk cloth

Tell Me All About It!

Ali Baba and the Forty Thieves

Adjectives are words that describe nouns. Adjectives tell what kind or how many. The words **a**, **an**, and **the** are special kinds of adjectives called **articles** that tell which one.

Examples:

what kind—**long** story

how many—**twenty** years

which one—**a** page

Read each sentence below. Circle each adjective in the sentence. There may be more than one in each sentence.

1. Cassim was a greedy man.

2. Ali Baba was a lowly woodcutter.

3. A huge rock covered the cave.

4. The captain said, "Open, sesame!" in a deep voice.

5. Ali Baba found amazing treasures.

6. Morgiana is a clever girl.

7. Ali Baba counted forty thieves near the large cave.

In number 7, which adjective tells which one?

In number 7, which adjective tells how many?

In number 7, which adjective tells what kind?

Say the Magic Words

Write the answer to each clue on the lines. Then, match the numbers, and use the letter above each number to fill in the answer to the riddle below.

Ali Baba
and the
Forty Thieves

The captain commanded forty of these _ _ _ _ _ _
                                                   2   7

Another word for weighing pan _ _ _ _ _
                              11   8

It made the coin stick to the weighing pan _ _ _ _ _
                                       9

Cassim was this to Ali Baba _ _ _ _ _ _ _
                            6

Animals used for carrying heavy loads _ _ _ _ _ _
                         10   1

How a thief marked Ali Baba's house _ _ _ _ _
                         4

These didn't hold oil, but thieves _ _ _ _
                    3

The captain was disguised as this _ _ _ _ _ _ _
             5

What does Ali Baba plant in his garden?

_ _ _ _ _ _   _ _ _ _ _
1 2 3 4 5 6   7 8 9 10 11

Treasure Map

Ali Baba has taken the treasure and buried it. Use the directions below to make a map on page 291 for Ali Baba to give to his son so he can find the treasure. Then, write out the directions to go from Ali Baba's house to the treasure.

Draw Ali Baba's house on the east side of the map.

Draw Cassim's house south of Ali Baba's house.

Draw some shops in the village west of the brothers' houses.

Draw the magic cave on the west side of the map.

Draw the forest surrounding the cave on the north, south, and east sides.

Draw some of the thieves east of the forest.

Now, make an **X** where you think Ali Baba might have hidden the treasure.

Directions from Ali Baba's house to the treasure:

Study Skills/Following Directions

Listen, Read, and Learn With Classic Stories, Grade 3

Study Skills/Following Directions

How Does the Story End?

What if Cassim had remembered the magic words and had been able to get out of the cave? What would have happened next? Use your imagination to write a new ending for the story in which Cassim escaped before the thieves returned. Draw a picture on another sheet of paper to illustrate your ending.

_____

_____

_____

_____

_____

_____

_____

_____

_____

Writing/Predicting a Story Ending   Listen, Read, and Learn With Classic Stories, Grade 3

Sign Correction Time

Read the following sign the oil merchant might have written and look for mistakes. Find and correct three capitalization mistakes, three punctuation mistakes, and two spelling mistakes.

omar the oil merchant will be in the

market next wednesday

Come early to buy your oil?

you don't want to be in the dark.

We have the best prices on oyl

in the marketplace

Look for the larje jars of oil.

.Ali Baba
and the
Forty Thieves

Reading Skills Checklist

Learning certain skills and strategies will help your child become a good reader. The following list shows the goals your child should reach in applying some basic skills during the third grade. Use the checklist after reading each story to assess your child's reading progress. Choose only a handful of skills to check at any one time. Sample questions have been given for each skill.

Skill	Rip Van Winkle	Fables	Anansi Learns to Fish	Brer Rabbit and the Tar Baby	John Henry: The Legend of a Steel-Driving Man	Ali Baba and the Forty Thieves
Author's Purpose Child can identify the reason for writing the story (to inform, persuade, express feeling, or entertain). *What do you think was the author's purpose in writing this story?*						
Cause and Effect Child can identify actions or events that either cause or result from other actions or events. *Why did the dog drop his bone?*						
Classify/Categorize Child can sort related words or objects into groups. *Which words are names of characters? Which characters are friendly? Which are unfriendly?*						
Compare and Contrast Child can identify similes and metaphors that help to compare and contrast. *What words or phrases does the author use to describe the two characters on this page?*						
Context Clues Child can use sentence and phonetic clues to help identify unfamiliar words. *Which word is unfamiliar? How can you figure out this word?*						
Draw Conclusions Child can use information from a story and from real life to draw conclusions that are not stated in the story. *How do you think Rip Van Winkle felt after he woke up?*						
Fact and Opinion Child can distinguish between statements of fact and statements of opinion. *Is this something you can prove or not? Is this something someone believes or thinks?*						
Main Idea and Details Child can identify the main idea and supporting details of a story or paragraph. *What is the main idea of the paragraph? Which sentences tell more about the main idea?*						

Skill	Rip Van Winkle	Fables	Anansi Learns to Fish	Brer Rabbit and the Tar Baby	John Henry: The Legend of a Steel-Driving Man	Ali Baba and the Forty Thieves
Making Judgments Child can decide what he or she thinks about the ideas in a story. *Do you think it was right for Ali Baba to take things from the thieves' cave? Why?*						
Predict Outcomes Child can make and modify predictions as he or she reads the story. The prediction need not be accurate, as long as it is generally consistent with what has happened so far in the story. *(during reading:) What do you think is going to happen to John Henry? Why do you think so? (after child reads a little more:) Do you still think that what you predicted is what will happen to John Henry, or do you want to change your prediction?*						
Reality/Fantasy Child can tell the difference between a realistic story and a fantasy. *Is this a realistic story? Why? Is this story a fantasy? Why?*						
Retell/Paraphrase Child can retell a story or an author's ideas in his or her own words. *How would you tell this story in your own words?*						
Character Child can describe characters and predict what they will do. *What is Brer Fox like?* *Do you think Anansi learned a lesson from what happened? Why or why not?*						
Plot Child can tell the major events of a story in order. *How did this story begin? What happened next? How did it end?*						
Setting Child can tell where and when a story takes place. *What is the setting of this story?*						
Summarize Child can describe the story in one or two sentences. *What is this story mostly about?*						
Visualize Child can form a mental picture of what happens in a story. *Which words help you picture the story in your mind as you read?*						

Answer Key

40 · What a Character!

The story tells many things about Rip Van Winkle. Use the words from the word box to complete the sentences.

kindness	lazy
nervous	confused
loveable	simple

1. Rip Van Winkle was not a very serious man. He lived a rather __simple__ life.

2. Rip showed much __kindness__ to his neighbors because he was always willing to help them.

3. Around his own home, though, Rip was __lazy__ and didn't do much work.

4. The village people were always glad to see Rip Van Winkle because they found him sweet and __loveable__.

5. When Rip was with the strange men playing ninepins, he felt uneasy and __nervous__.

6. When Rip woke up, he didn't realized he'd slept so long. He was __confused__ when nothing looked the same.

41 · Tell Me Again

Cut out the pictures here and on page 43. Put the story cards in order. Number them from 1 to 8. Then, glue each picture to a half sheet of construction paper. On each page, write what is happening in the story to describe the picture. Now, you have your own mini-book.

43 · Tell Me Again (page 2)

Sample answers: Rip sneaks away to the mountains. He helps an old man carry a barrel of cider. Rip meets strange men playing ninepins. He drinks cider and falls asleep. Rip wakes up much older. He goes home, but his home is gone. He meets his grown-up daughter and son. Rip lives with his daughter and her family.

45 · Plot It Out

The **plot** is what happens in a story. Use the chart below to record the plot of "Rip Van Winkle." Then, use the events to summarize the main thing that happens in the story. Make the summary only one or two sentences long.

Sample answers: **Rip Van Winkle**

Beginning	Middle	End
Rip Van Winkle goes for a walk in the mountains. He sees strange men playing ninepins and drinks their cider.	Rip Van Winkle falls asleep in the mountains.	Rip Van Winkle wakes up and returns to the village. Everything has changed. He discovers that he has slept 20 years. He goes to live with his daughter.

Summary

Rip Van Winkle returns to his village after sleeping for 20 years in the mountains.

46

A Place in Time

The **setting** is the place and time in which a story happens. Think about the setting of "Rip Van Winkle." Read each question below and answer it by writing **yes** or **no**. Then, write a brief description of the setting of "Rip Van Winkle."

1. Does the story take place in modern times? __no__

2. Does the story take place in what is now the state of Florida? __no__

3. Does the story take place in the mountains? __yes__

4. Does the story take place in a large city? __no__

The story "Rip Van Winkle" takes place _Sample answer:_ _long ago in what is now the state of New York. Part of_ _the story happens when Rip is in the mountains. Other_ _parts happen in his village._

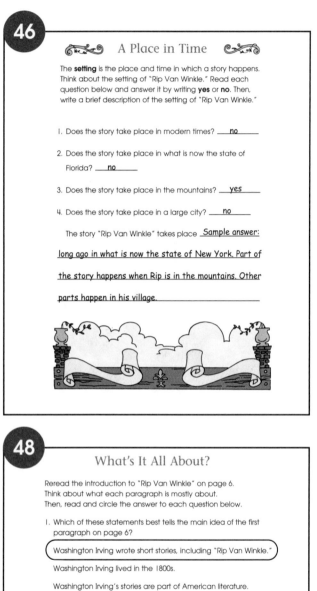

47

More Confusion

Read each sentence. Underline one word in each sentence that makes the sentence not true. Change the sentence by replacing the underlined word with a word from the list. Write the new sentence.

> thunderstorm   years   mountains   village   watch

1. The legend of Rip Van Winkle takes place long ago in the desert near the Hudson River. _The legend of Rip Van Winkle_ _takes place long ago in the mountains near the Hudson River._

2. When Rip walked through the mountains with the strange man, he heard rumbling he thought was an earthquake. _When Rip walked through the mountains with the strange_ _man, he heard rumbling he thought was a thunderstorm._

3. When Rip woke up, he reached for his money, but only found rusted bits of metal. _When Rip woke up, he reached_ _for his watch, but only found rusted bits of metal._

4. As Rip returned to the library, he found people were staring at him. _As Rip returned to the village, he found people_ _were staring at him._

5. After talking to people, Rip discovered that twenty minutes had passed for him as if they had been one night. _After talking to people, Rip discovered that twenty years_ _had passed for him as if they had been one night._

48

What's It All About?

Reread the introduction to "Rip Van Winkle" on page 6. Think about what each paragraph is mostly about. Then, read and circle the answer to each question below.

1. Which of these statements best tells the main idea of the first paragraph on page 6?

   (Washington Irving wrote short stories, including "Rip Van Winkle.")

   Washington Irving lived in the 1800s.

   Washington Irving's stories are part of American literature.

2. Which of these statements best tells the main idea of the second paragraph on page 6?

   Henry Hudson was an English explorer.

   New York was important for Dutch settlers.

   ("Rip Van Winkle" takes place in a Dutch settlement in New York just before the American Revolution.)

3. Which of these statements best tells the main idea of the last paragraph on page 6?

   A boy sleeps in a cave for 57 years.

   (The story of "Rip Van Winkle" is like a story told on Crete.)

   A boy looks for sheep after a nap.

4. What is another good title for page 6?

   Possible answers: Rip Van Winkle and Its Author; _Washington Irving and the Tale of Rip Van Winkle_

49

Reality or Fantasy?

When story events could really happen, they are called **reality**. When story events could not really happen, they are called **fantasy**. Read the following story events from "Rip Van Winkle" and think about whether or not they could really happen. Write each event in the correct place on the chart.

- Rip Van Winkle fell asleep in the mountains.
- Rip Van Winkle heard thunder that was really men playing ninepins.
- Rip Van Winkle slept for twenty years.
- Rip Van Winkle grew old.
- Rip Van Winkle returned to his village.

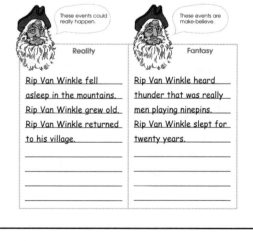

Reality	Fantasy
Rip Van Winkle fell asleep in the mountains. Rip Van Winkle grew old. Rip Van Winkle returned to his village.	Rip Van Winkle heard thunder that was really men playing ninepins. Rip Van Winkle slept for twenty years.

These events could really happen.

These events are make-believe.

50 — Interesting Actions

Verbs are words that show action. Some verbs are more exact and give the reader more information. Read the following examples. Notice that a more exact verb is used in the second sentence.

Rip Van Winkle <u>looked</u> at the strange man.

Rip Van Winkle <u>gazed</u> at the strange man.

Read the following sentences. Replace the underlined verb with one that is more exact. Write it in the blank. Several answers are possible.

Possible answers:

1. Rip <u>walked</u> in the mountains. __hiked, wandered, strolled__

2. Wolf <u>ran</u> to Rip. __dashed, rushed, hurried__

3. "You are so lazy!" Rip's wife <u>said</u>. __yelled, screamed, nagged__

4. Rip <u>drank</u> some cider. __sipped, gulped, guzzled__

5. Rip <u>looked</u> for his watch. __searched, hunted__

6. When Rip returned to the village, he <u>told</u> his story. __explained, described__

51 — What Is the Meaning of This?

Read each sentence. Choose the correct meaning of the underlined word. Circle the answer.

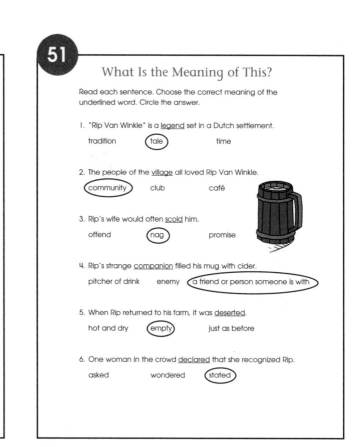

1. "Rip Van Winkle" is a <u>legend</u> set in a Dutch settlement.
   tradition   (tale)   time

2. The people of the <u>village</u> all loved Rip Van Winkle.
   (community)   club   café

3. Rip's wife would often <u>scold</u> him.
   offend   (nag)   promise

4. Rip's strange <u>companion</u> filled his mug with cider.
   pitcher of drink   enemy   (a friend or person someone is with)

5. When Rip returned to his farm, it was <u>deserted</u>.
   hot and dry   (empty)   just as before

6. One woman in the crowd <u>declared</u> that she recognized Rip.
   asked   wondered   (stated)

52 — Rip's Journal Entry

Think about Rip Van Winkle's experience when he came back from the mountains. Complete the following sentences as if you are Rip Van Winkle writing a journal entry.

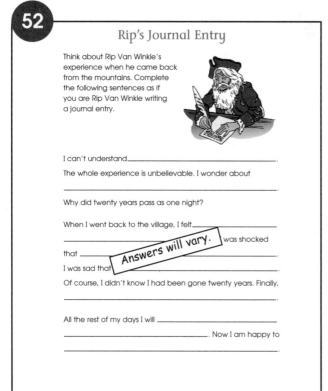

I can't understand_____.

The whole experience is unbelievable. I wonder about
_____

Why did twenty years pass as one night?

When I went back to the village, I felt _____

that _____ *Answers will vary.* ____ was shocked

I was sad that _____

Of course, I didn't know I had been gone twenty years. Finally,
_____

All the rest of my days I will _____
_____. Now I am happy to
_____.

53 — People and Places

Words that name people, places, or things are **nouns**. Words that name special people, places, or things are **proper nouns**. Proper nouns begin with capital letters. Read these examples.

Black Hills

the Great Lakes

George Washington Carver

Find the proper noun in each sentence. Rewrite it with one or more capital letters.

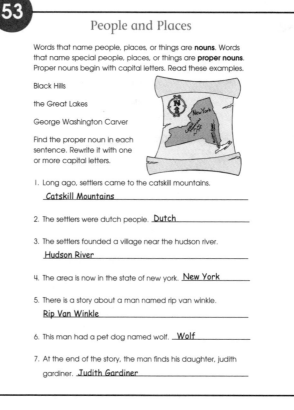

1. Long ago, settlers came to the catskill mountains.
   __Catskill Mountains__

2. The settlers were dutch people. __Dutch__

3. The settlers founded a village near the hudson river.
   __Hudson River__

4. The area is now in the state of new york. __New York__

5. There is a story about a man named rip van winkle.
   __Rip Van Winkle__

6. This man had a pet dog named wolf. __Wolf__

7. At the end of the story, the man finds his daughter, judith gardiner. __Judith Gardiner__

88

What's the Point?

A **fable** is a story that teaches a lesson. Complete the chart by writing a summary of what happens in each story. Then, choose the lesson from the list below that fits the story. Write the letter of the lesson in the last column. Not all the choices will be used.

a. Things may not turn out the way you think they will.

b. Don't wait until tomorrow to do what you can do today.

c. You have to put all the parts of the story together to get the whole story.

d. In times of trouble, use your head to find a solution to the problem.

e. Don't lose everything you have because you wish for what others have.

Title	Summary	Lesson
1. The Blind Men and the Elephant	Six blind men touch different parts of an elephant. They all think an elephant is something different because of the part they touched. In the end, they realize that the elephant is made up of many parts.	c
2. The Dog and His Bone	A dog holding his bone sees his reflection in a pond. He thinks it is another dog. He dicides to take the other dog's bone away and ends up losing his.	e
3. The Milkmaid and Her Pail	As the milkmaid is taking her milk to sell it, she plans how she is going to make money to buy fancy clothes. She isn't careful and spills the milk. Then she gets no money because she has nothing to sell.	a

89

Front-Page News

Picture yourself as a reporter. Imagine that you have interviewed one or more of the blind men, Pup, or Molly the milkmaid. Write a news article based on the facts you have gathered.

1. Record your interview notes on the notebook page below.

2. Write your story on a separate sheet of paper. Give details that tell who, what, when, where, and why.

3. Draw a picture that shows an important event in the story.

Notes

Answers will vary.

90

Words to Watch

Read each meaning. Find a word from the box that matches the meaning. Write the word on the line.

pranced	scorching	blossoms
peered	task	reflection
trudged	valuable	commotion

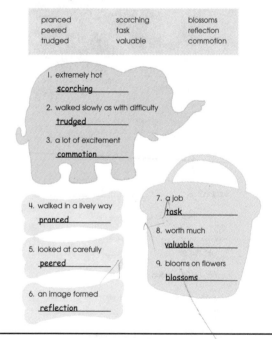

1. extremely hot
   scorching

2. walked slowly as with difficulty
   trudged

3. a lot of excitement
   commotion

4. walked in a lively way
   pranced

5. looked at carefully
   peered

6. an image formed
   reflection

7. a job
   task

8. worth much
   valuable

9. blooms on flowers
   blossoms

91

Character Forecast

When you **predict** what a character might do or what might happen next in a story, you use clues from what you've read. Make a prediction about each fable. Read the question and circle the best answer. Then, list the clues you used from the story to make the prediction.

1. What do you think Pup will do the next time he sees something he'd like to have?
   a. try to get it away from the owner
   b. appreciate what he has
   c. go to sleep

Clues: _He lost his bone because he was trying to get another one. He probably learned a lesson and won't try that again._

2. What do you think Molly the milkmaid will do the next time she makes plans about the future?
   a. pay attention to what she is doing at the time so her plans are not spoiled
   b. tell everyone she knows about her plans because she is sure they will happen
   c. worry about her plans until they happen

Clues: _Her plans didn't happen because she wasn't careful about what she was doing. She will probably be careful next time._

3. What do you think the blind men will do the next time they explore something new?
   a. explore just one part of the thing
   b. choose one of them to do all the exploring
   c. make sure they think about all the parts instead of just one

Clues: _The blind men learned that the elephant was made up of many parts. Next time, they will think about all the parts._

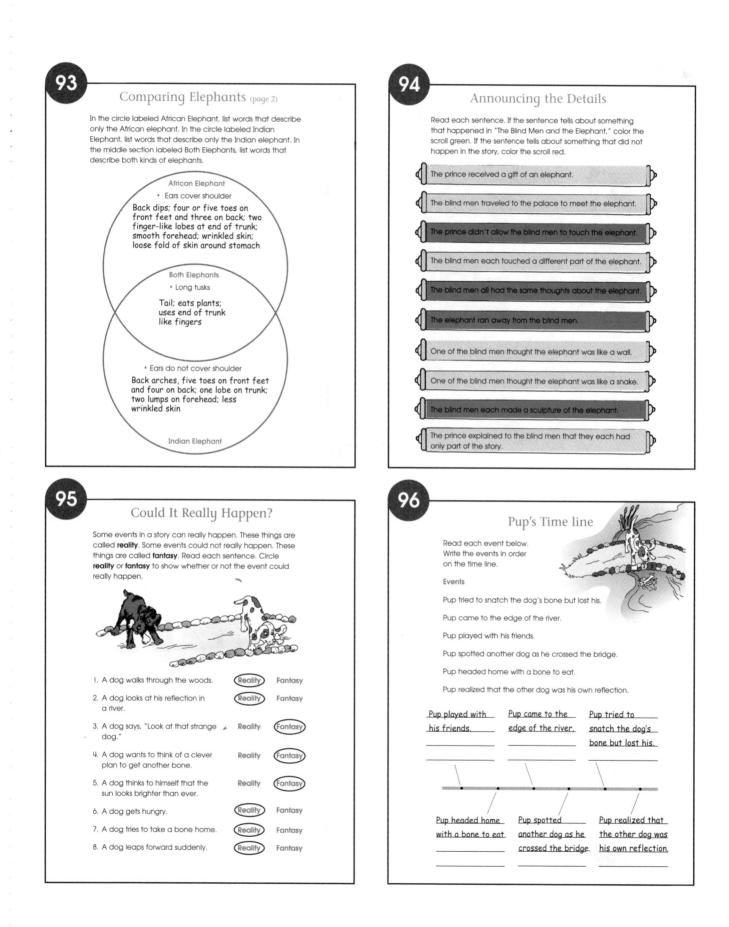

93

Comparing Elephants (page 2)

In the circle labeled African Elephant, list words that describe only the African elephant. In the circle labeled Indian Elephant, list words that describe only the Indian elephant. In the middle section labeled Both Elephants, list words that describe both kinds of elephants.

African Elephant
• Ears cover shoulder
Back dips; four or five toes on front feet and three on back; two finger-like lobes at end of trunk; smooth forehead; wrinkled skin; loose fold of skin around stomach

Both Elephants
• Long tusks
Tail; eats plants; uses end of trunk like fingers

• Ears do not cover shoulder
Back arches, five toes on front feet and four on back; one lobe on trunk; two lumps on forehead; less wrinkled skin

Indian Elephant

94

Announcing the Details

Read each sentence. If the sentence tells about something that happened in "The Blind Men and the Elephant," color the scroll green. If the sentence tells about something that did not happen in the story, color the scroll red.

The prince received a gift of an elephant.

The blind men traveled to the palace to meet the elephant.

The prince didn't allow the blind men to touch the elephant.

The blind men each touched a different part of the elephant.

The blind men all had the same thoughts about the elephant.

The elephant ran away from the blind men.

One of the blind men thought the elephant was like a wall.

One of the blind men thought the elephant was like a snake.

The blind men each made a sculpture of the elephant.

The prince explained to the blind men that they each had only part of the story.

95

Could It Really Happen?

Some events in a story can really happen. These things are called **reality**. Some events could not really happen. These things are called **fantasy**. Read each sentence. Circle **reality** or **fantasy** to show whether or not the event could really happen.

1. A dog walks through the woods. (Reality) Fantasy
2. A dog looks at his reflection in a river. (Reality) Fantasy
3. A dog says, "Look at that strange dog." Reality (Fantasy)
4. A dog wants to think of a clever plan to get another bone. Reality (Fantasy)
5. A dog thinks to himself that the sun looks brighter than ever. Reality (Fantasy)
6. A dog gets hungry. (Reality) Fantasy
7. A dog tries to take a bone home. (Reality) Fantasy
8. A dog leaps forward suddenly. (Reality) Fantasy

96

Pup's Time line

Read each event below. Write the events in order on the time line.

Events

Pup tried to snatch the dog's bone but lost his.

Pup came to the edge of the river.

Pup played with his friends.

Pup spotted another dog as he crossed the bridge.

Pup headed home with a bone to eat.

Pup realized that the other dog was his own reflection.

Pup played with his friends. | Pup came to the edge of the river. | Pup tried to snatch the dog's bone but lost his.

Pup headed home with a bone to eat. | Pup spotted another dog as he crossed the bridge. | Pup realized that the other dog was his own reflection.

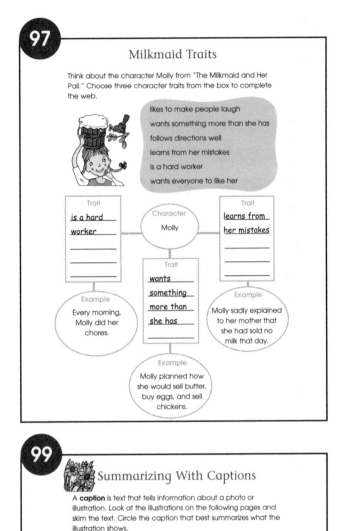

97 — Milkmaid Traits

Think about the character Molly from "The Milkmaid and Her Pail." Choose three character traits from the box to complete the web.

likes to make people laugh

wants something more than she has

follows directions well

learns from her mistakes

is a hard worker

wants everyone to like her

Trait: is a hard worker

Character: Molly

Trait: learns from her mistakes

Trait: wants something more than she has

Example: Every morning, Molly did her chores.

Example: Molly sadly explained to her mother that she had sold no milk that day.

Example: Molly planned how she would sell butter, buy eggs, and sell chickens.

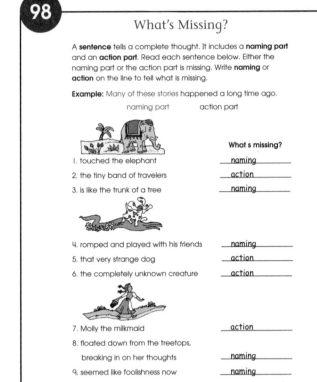

98 — What's Missing?

A **sentence** tells a complete thought. It includes a **naming part** and an **action part**. Read each sentence below. Either the naming part or the action part is missing. Write **naming** or **action** on the line to tell what is missing.

Example: Many of these stories happened a long time ago.

naming part   action part

What's missing?

1. touched the elephant — naming
2. the tiny band of travelers — action
3. is like the trunk of a tree — naming

4. romped and played with his friends — naming
5. that very strange dog — action
6. the completely unknown creature — action

7. Molly the milkmaid — action
8. floated down from the treetops, breaking in on her thoughts — naming
9. seemed like foolishness now — naming

99 — Summarizing With Captions

A **caption** is text that tells information about a photo or illustration. Look at the illustrations on the following pages and skim the text. Circle the caption that best summarizes what the illustration shows.

Page 79

Molly is a happy girl.

(Molly goes to milk the cow each day.)

Molly has a cow.

Pages 80—81

Molly gets exercise every day.

Molly likes flowers.

(Molly takes the milk to town to sell it.)

Page 82

(Molly gets an idea from a canary.)

Molly is a pretty girl.

Molly carries the pail on her head.

Page 83

Molly is tired of carrying the milk.

(Molly has grand plans for herself in fancy clothes.)

Molly wants to go home.

Page 84

Molly thinks of a way to save the milk.

Molly is practicing her dance steps.

(Molly is sad because she spilled the milk.)

Page 85

Molly's mother tells her to sweep the cottage.

(Molly explains to her mother what happened.)

Molly and her mother have to move to a new cottage.

100 — A Careful Reading

Read the following text that might appear on the book jackets of the fables. For each story, find and correct two capitalization mistakes, two punctuation mistakes, and two spelling mistakes. Make your corrections above each mistake or within the paragraph.

The Blind Men and the Elephant

What does an elefant look like? That is the question six men who are blind want to answer. To do so, they touch an elephant. the problem is, each touches a different part and has a different idea about what an elephant is like. With help from a prince, the men figure out that they have to put all the parts together to get the complete store.

101

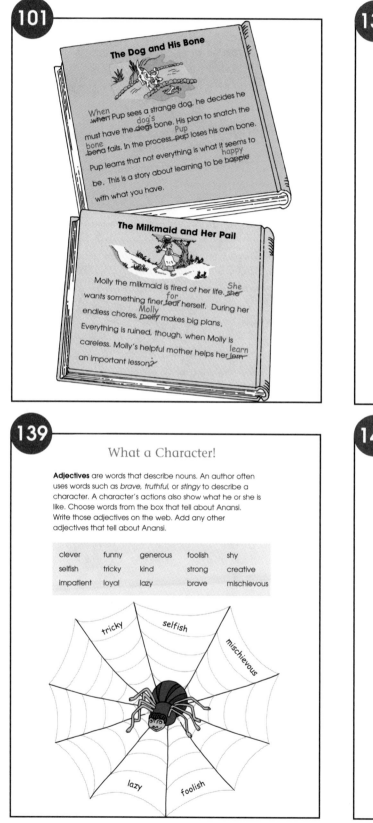

The Dog and His Bone

When
~~When~~ Pup sees a strange dog, he decides he
dog's
must have the ~~dogs~~ bone. His plan to snatch the
bone   *Pup*
~~bena~~ fails. In the process, ~~pup~~ loses his own bone.
Pup learns that not everything is what it seems to
happy
be. This is a story about learning to be ~~happie~~

with what you have.

The Milkmaid and Her Pail

She
Molly the milkmaid is tired of her life. ~~she~~
for
wants something finer ~~four~~ herself. During her
Molly
endless chores, ~~molly~~ makes big plans.

Everything is ruined, though, when Molly is
learn
careless. Molly's helpful mother helps her ~~lem~~
an important lesson.~~?~~

136

Well Noted

Read the following note Turtle might have written to Anansi.
Find and correct three capitalization mistakes, three
punctuation mistakes, and two spelling mistakes. Insert the end
punctuation where needed. Make the capitalization and
spelling corrections above the type.

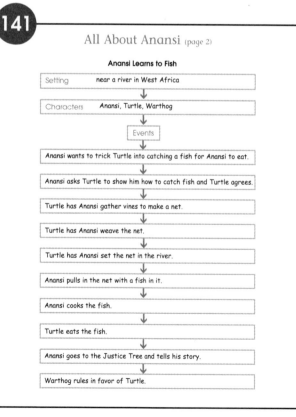

Anansi,
Dear ~~anansi~~
I
~~i~~ am sorry for what I have done. It wasn't very
way
nice to trick you that ~~weay~~. I would like to try again
to be your friend. Would you please come over for
It
dinner~~,~~ ? I would like to cook some fish for you. ~~it~~ will
make up for the one I ate without sharing. If you
fun
could come for dinner, I think it would be ~~fune~~.

Your friend,

Turtle

139

What a Character!

Adjectives are words that describe nouns. An author often
uses words such as *brave, truthful,* or *stingy* to describe a
character. A character's actions also show what he or she is
like. Choose words from the box that tell about Anansi.
Write those adjectives on the web. Add any other
adjectives that tell about Anansi.

clever	funny	generous	foolish	shy
selfish	tricky	kind	strong	creative
impatient	loyal	lazy	brave	mischievous

tricky   selfish   mischievous

lazy   foolish

141

All About Anansi (page 2)

Anansi Learns to Fish

Setting	near a river in West Africa

↓

Characters	Anansi, Turtle, Warthog

↓

Events

↓

Anansi wants to trick Turtle into catching a fish for Anansi to eat.

↓

Anansi asks Turtle to show him how to catch fish and Turtle agrees.

↓

Turtle has Anansi gather vines to make a net.

↓

Turtle has Anansi weave the net.

↓

Turtle has Anansi set the net in the river.

↓

Anansi pulls in the net with a fish in it.

↓

Anansi cooks the fish.

↓

Turtle eats the fish.

↓

Anansi goes to the Justice Tree and tells his story.

↓

Warthog rules in favor of Turtle.

143

Main Idea
Turtle tricks Anansi.

⑤   Supporting Detail
Turtle says that one can eat the fish while the other gets full. Anansi says he wants to get full, so Turtle eats all the fish.

④   Supporting Detail
Turtle says that he will cook the fish, but Anansi wants to eat it all himself so he does it. Turtle sleeps.

③   Supporting Detail
Turtle says that this time he will do the work, but Anansi says that is the hardest part. Turtle rests again.

②   Supporting Detail
Turtle says that one can work hard and the other can get tired. Anansi doesn't want to get tired. Turtle sleeps.

①   Supporting Detail
Turtle says that one of them can work hard and one can get scratched. Anansi doesn't wnat to get scratched. Turtle rests.

144

Justice Rules

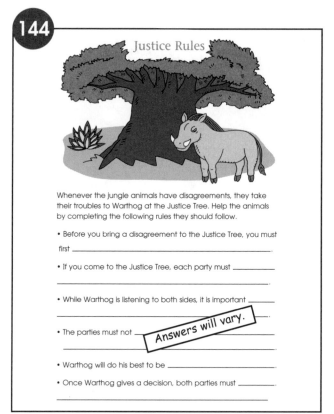

Whenever the jungle animals have disagreements, they take their troubles to Warthog at the Justice Tree. Help the animals by completing the following rules they should follow.

• Before you bring a disagreement to the Justice Tree, you must first _____.

• If you come to the Justice Tree, each party must _____

• While Warthog is listening to both sides, it is important _____

_____

• The parties must not *Answers will vary.*

_____

• Warthog will do his best to be _____

• Once Warthog gives a decision, both parties must _____.

_____

145

Web of Words

Read each definition. Cut out the words at the bottom of the page. Match each word by gluing it to the space with its definition.

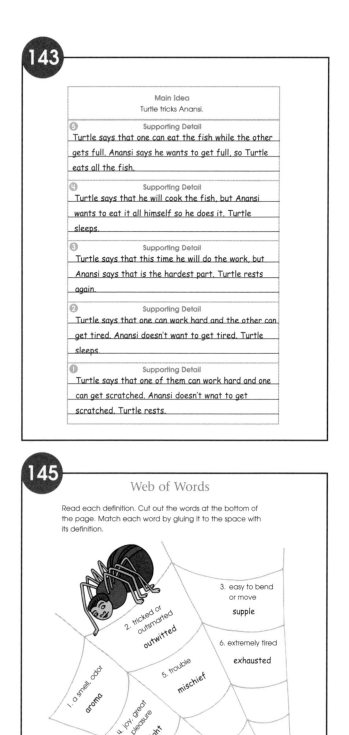

3. easy to bend or move
supple

6. extremely tired
exhausted

2. tricked or outsmarted
outwitted

5. trouble
mischief

1. a smell, odor
aroma

4. joy, great pleasure
delight

delight	exhausted	supple
mischief	aroma	outwitted

147

Fine Points

Read each question about the story. Answer in your own words.

1. At the beginning of the story, what does Anansi set out to do?
He plans to trick Turtle into catching a fish for him to eat.

2. Why does Anansi not want to get scratched?
He has too many arms and legs.

3. What does Turtle do each time while Anansi does the work?
He rests or sleeps.

4. When does Anansi realize he's been tricked? _____
He knows he's been tricked after Turtle has eaten all the fish.

5. What does Anansi do to get back at Turtle? _____
He goes to see Warthog at the Justice Tree.

6. What does Warthog say about Anansi's story? Warthog says that Anansi's story about him doing all the work and Turtle getting tired is nonsense. He tells Anansi to go home.

148

Collection of Words

At the beginning of the story, the author uses the words **big** and **huge** to describe Turtle's fish. These two words are synonyms. **Synonyms** are words that mean almost the same thing. Toward the end of the story, Anansi is **hungry** and Turtle is **full**. These two words are antonyms. **Antonyms** are words that mean the opposite of one another.

Think about synonyms and antonyms. Read the following clues, and write a word from the box.

friend	edge	scream
young	gather	together
simple	tired	tomorrow

1. Synonym for weary ___tired___
2. Synonym for easy ___simple___
3. Synonym for pal ___friend___
4. Synonym for shriek ___scream___
5. Antonym for middle ___edge___
6. Antonym for scatter ___gather___
7. Antonym for yesterday ___tomorrow___
8. Antonym for alone ___together___

Write one sentence using two antonyms.
___Answers will vary.___

149

Compare With Flair

In "Anansi Learns to Fish," Anansi thinks that fooling Turtle will be as simple as making a hyena laugh. The author uses the word **as** to compare two actions—fooling Turtle and making a hyena laugh. In other words, the spider thinks that his friend can be easily tricked. Any comparison that uses the word **as** or **like** is called a **simile** (SIHM uh lee).

Write a word or phrase from the box to complete each simile below.

honey	delicate white lace	an empty barrel	an arrow

1. The hungry spider felt as hollow as ___an empty barrel___.
2. The fish moved through the water like ___an arrow___.
3. The spider's web looked like ___delicate white lace___.
4. The melon tasted as sweet as ___honey___.

Now, try writing your own similes. Choose something to describe. Then, think of something that it can be compared with. Start with these phrases or use your own ideas.
Answers will vary.
The campfire was as bright as _____.

Those giraffes are as tall as _____.

The parrot sounded like _____.

184

Sticky Points—Details

Read each sentence. If the details were part of the story, write **yes**. If the details were not part of the story, write **no**.

1. Brer Fox tied himself to a bull's tail. ___no___

2. Brer Fox put a Tar Baby in the briar patch. ___no___

3. The Tar Baby said hello to Brer Rabbit, but it was really Brer Fox talking from the bushes. ___no___

4. Brer Rabbit ended up with his hands, feet, and head stuck to the Tar Baby. ___yes___

5. Brer Fox asked his mother what he should do with Brer Rabbit. ___no___

6. Brer Fox said he wouldn't barbecue Brer Rabbit because he forgot how to make his sauce. ___no___

7. Brer Rabbit said that he'd rather get his ears wet in the pond than be thrown in the briar patch. ___yes___

8. Brer Fox threw Brer Rabbit into the pond. ___no___

185

Summing Up "Brer Rabbit"

Think about the story. Complete the summary chart to tell what the story was mostly about. Use the chart to tell someone who hasn't read "Brer Rabbit" about the story.

Brer Rabbit

Characters
Who is the story about?
Brer Rabbit, Brer Fox

Setting
Where does the story take place?
In the country, near a briar patch

Summary
What are the main events that happen in the story?
Brer Fox wants to pay back Brer Rabbit for tricks that have been played on him. Brer Fox makes a Tar Baby and Brer Rabbit gets stuck to it. Brer Fox says this is the end of Brer Rabbit. But Brer Rabbit tricks Brer Fox again. This time he makes him think that being put in the briar patch would be the worst thing. Brer Fox falls for the trick and Brer Rabbit gets away.

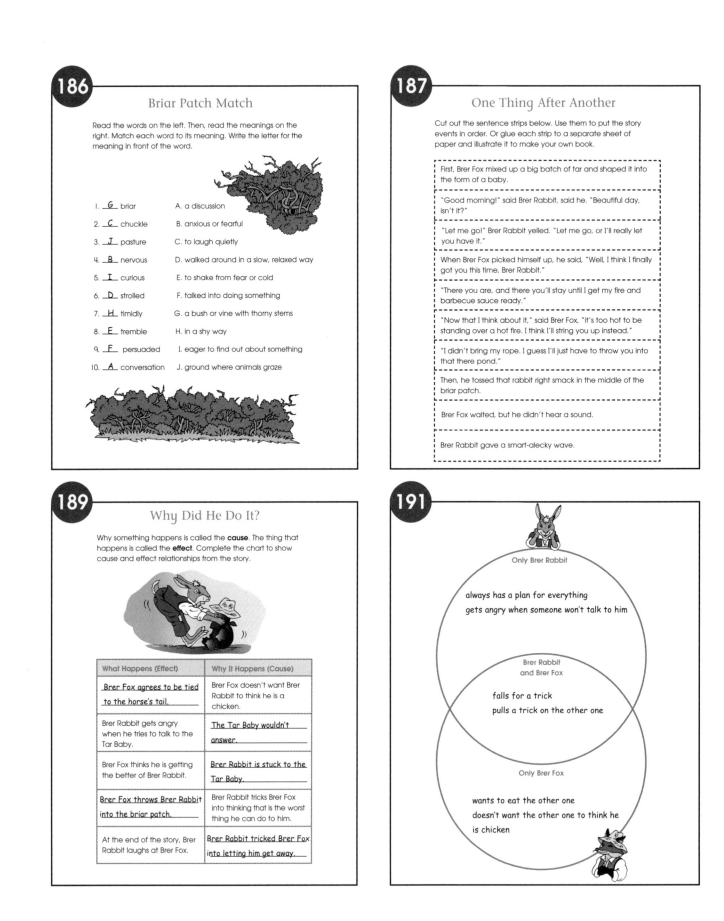

186

Briar Patch Match

Read the words on the left. Then, read the meanings on the right. Match each word to its meaning. Write the letter for the meaning in front of the word.

1. _G_ briar   A. a discussion
2. _C_ chuckle   B. anxious or fearful
3. _J_ pasture   C. to laugh quietly
4. _B_ nervous   D. walked around in a slow, relaxed way
5. _I_ curious   E. to shake from fear or cold
6. _D_ strolled   F. talked into doing something
7. _H_ timidly   G. a bush or vine with thorny stems
8. _E_ tremble   H. in a shy way
9. _F_ persuaded   I. eager to find out about something
10. _A_ conversation J. ground where animals graze

187

One Thing After Another

Cut out the sentence strips below. Use them to put the story events in order. Or glue each strip to a separate sheet of paper and illustrate it to make your own book.

First, Brer Fox mixed up a big batch of tar and shaped it into the form of a baby.

"Good morning!" said Brer Rabbit, said he. "Beautiful day, isn't it?"

"Let me go!" Brer Rabbit yelled. "Let me go, or I'll really let you have it."

When Brer Fox picked himself up, he said, "Well, I think I finally got you this time, Brer Rabbit."

"There you are, and there you'll stay until I get my fire and barbecue sauce ready."

"Now that I think about it," said Brer Fox, "it's too hot to be standing over a hot fire. I think I'll string you up instead."

"I didn't bring my rope. I guess I'll just have to throw you into that there pond."

Then, he tossed that rabbit right smack in the middle of the briar patch.

Brer Fox waited, but he didn't hear a sound.

Brer Rabbit gave a smart-alecky wave.

189

Why Did He Do It?

Why something happens is called the **cause**. The thing that happens is called the **effect**. Complete the chart to show cause and effect relationships from the story.

What Happens (Effect)	Why It Happens (Cause)
Brer Fox agrees to be tied to the horse's tail.	Brer Fox doesn't want Brer Rabbit to think he is a chicken.
Brer Rabbit gets angry when he tries to talk to the Tar Baby.	The Tar Baby wouldn't answer.
Brer Fox thinks he is getting the better of Brer Rabbit.	Brer Rabbit is stuck to the Tar Baby.
Brer Fox throws Brer Rabbit into the briar patch.	Brer Rabbit tricks Brer Fox into thinking that is the worst thing he can do to him.
At the end of the story, Brer Rabbit laughs at Brer Fox.	Brer Rabbit tricked Brer Fox into letting him get away.

191

Only Brer Rabbit

always has a plan for everything
gets angry when someone won't talk to him

Brer Rabbit and Brer Fox

falls for a trick
pulls a trick on the other one

Only Brer Fox

wants to eat the other one
doesn't want the other one to think he is chicken

What If?

The **point of view** of a story comes from the character telling the story. "Brer Rabbit and the Tar Baby" is told by someone who is not a character in the story. This is known as **third-person** point of view. The story is told using the pronouns **he**, **she**, and **they**. In a story told from the **first-person** point of view, the narrator (the person telling the story) is usually a character in the story. The narrator uses the pronouns **I** and **me** when talking about himself or herself, but can use the pronouns **he**, **she**, and **they** when talking about other characters in the story.

What if Brer Rabbit, Brer Fox, or even the Tar Baby told the story Brer Rabbit and the Tar Baby"? Choose a part of the story. Rewrite it using the first-person point of view. If you need more space, continue on a separate sheet of paper.

"Here's the real story. . . ."

Answers will vary.

Picture This

The illustrations for a story can give you clues about what is happening in the story. Look at the illustrations on the pages listed below. Then, answer each question.

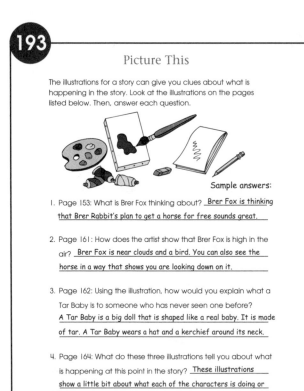

Sample answers:

1. Page 153: What is Brer Fox thinking about? _Brer Fox is thinking that Brer Rabbit's plan to get a horse for free sounds great._

2. Page 161: How does the artist show that Brer Fox is high in the air? _Brer Fox is near clouds and a bird. You can also see the horse in a way that shows you are looking down on it._

3. Page 162: Using the illustration, how would you explain what a Tar Baby is to someone who has never seen one before? _A Tar Baby is a big doll that is shaped like a real baby. It is made of tar. A Tar Baby wears a hat and a kerchief around its neck._

4. Page 164: What do these three illustrations tell you about what is happening at this point in the story? _These illustrations show a little bit about what each of the characters is doing or feeling._

Sounds Around

The **ou** sound can stand for more than one sound. Read the list of story words. Sort the words by writing each word in the correct column.

| ground | shout | bouncing | around |
| sound | could | louder | would |

ou as in **found**

ground
sound
shout
bouncing
louder
around

ou as in **should**

could
would

Hop on Opposites

Brer Rabbit told Brer Fox to hold on **tight** to the horse, but later he wanted the Tar Baby to turn him **loose**. **Antonyms** are words that have opposite meanings, such as **tight** and **loose**. Read the first word in each line. Then, draw a line to show how Brer Rabbit might hop from the first word to its opposite as in the example below.

tight	close	happy	strong	loose
1. **up**	high	down	near	above
2. **old**	new	far	worn	clean
3. **shout**	yell	whisper	ask	cry
4. **top**	middle	highest	bottom	even
5. **first**	leading	best	last	worst
6. **quiet**	careful	silent	calm	loud
7. **strong**	weak	brave	solid	firm
8. **wrong**	incorrect	bad	hurtful	right
9. **stop**	quit	end	begin	leave
10. **big**	large	small	huge	roomy

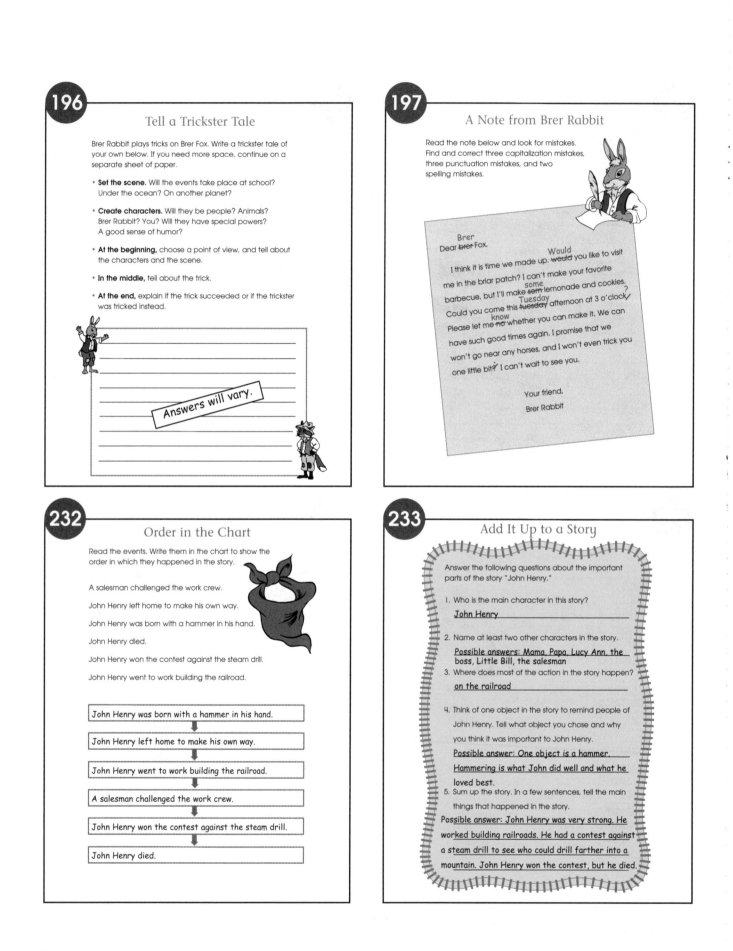

196

Tell a Trickster Tale

Brer Rabbit plays tricks on Brer Fox. Write a trickster tale of your own below. If you need more space, continue on a separate sheet of paper.

- **Set the scene.** Will the events take place at school? Under the ocean? On another planet?

- **Create characters.** Will they be people? Animals? Brer Rabbit? You? Will they have special powers? A good sense of humor?

- **At the beginning,** choose a point of view, and tell about the characters and the scene.

- **In the middle,** tell about the trick.

- **At the end,** explain if the trick succeeded or if the trickster was tricked instead.

Answers will vary.

197

A Note from Brer Rabbit

Read the note below and look for mistakes. Find and correct three capitalization mistakes, three punctuation mistakes, and two spelling mistakes.

Brer
Dear ~~brer~~ Fox,

                                    Would
I think it is time we made up. ~~would~~ you like to visit
me in the briar patch? I can't make your favorite
                            some
barbecue, but I'll make ~~som~~ lemonade and cookies.
                        Tuesday   ?
Could you come this ~~tuesday~~ afternoon at 3 o'clock
            know
Please let me ~~no~~ whether you can make it. We can
have such good times again. I promise that we
won't go near any horses, and I won't even trick you
one little bit? I can't wait to see you.

                    Your friend,
                    Brer Rabbit

232

Order in the Chart

Read the events. Write them in the chart to show the order in which they happened in the story.

A salesman challenged the work crew.

John Henry left home to make his own way.

John Henry was born with a hammer in his hand.

John Henry died.

John Henry won the contest against the steam drill.

John Henry went to work building the railroad.

| John Henry was born with a hammer in his hand. |
| John Henry left home to make his own way. |
| John Henry went to work building the railroad. |
| A salesman challenged the work crew. |
| John Henry won the contest against the steam drill. |
| John Henry died. |

233

Add It Up to a Story

Answer the following questions about the important parts of the story "John Henry."

1. Who is the main character in this story?
   <u>John Henry</u>

2. Name at least two other characters in the story.
   <u>Possible answers: Mama, Papa, Lucy Ann, the boss, Little Bill, the salesman</u>

3. Where does most of the action in the story happen?
   <u>on the railroad</u>

4. Think of one object in the story to remind people of John Henry. Tell what object you chose and why you think it was important to John Henry.
   <u>Possible answer: One object is a hammer. Hammering is what John did well and what he loved best.</u>

5. Sum up the story. In a few sentences, tell the main things that happened in the story.
   <u>Possible answer: John Henry was very strong. He worked building railroads. He had a contest against a steam drill to see who could drill farther into a mountain. John Henry won the contest, but he died.</u>

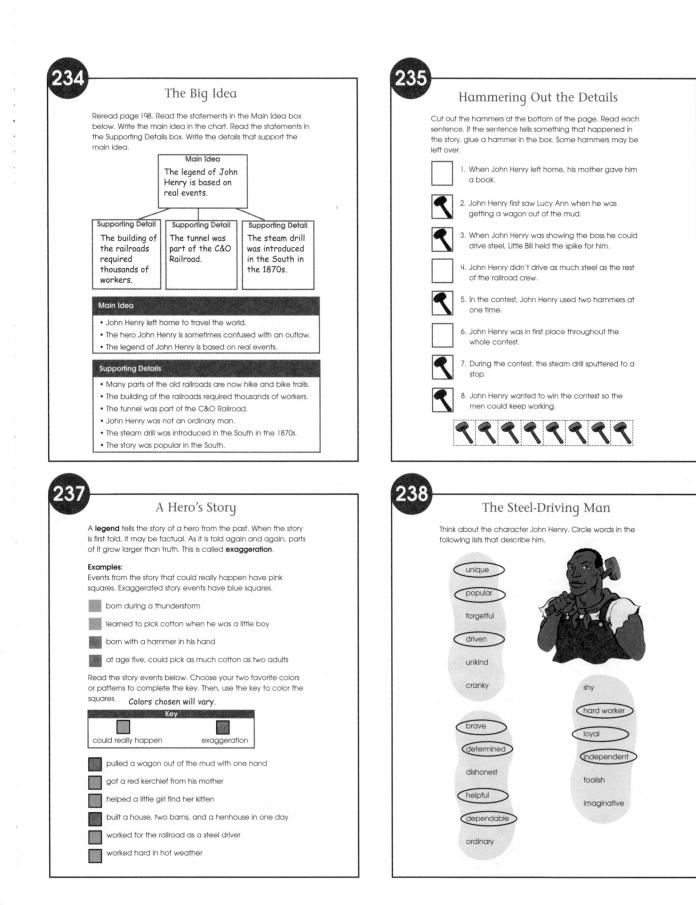

234

The Big Idea

Reread page 198. Read the statements in the Main Idea box below. Write the main idea in the chart. Read the statements in the Supporting Details box. Write the details that support the main idea.

Main Idea

The legend of John Henry is based on real events.

Supporting Detail

The building of the railroads required thousands of workers.

Supporting Detail

The tunnel was part of the C&O Railroad.

Supporting Detail

The steam drill was introduced in the South in the 1870s.

Main Idea

- John Henry left home to travel the world.
- The hero John Henry is sometimes confused with an outlaw.
- The legend of John Henry is based on real events.

Supporting Details

- Many parts of the old railroads are now hike and bike trails.
- The building of the railroads required thousands of workers.
- The tunnel was part of the C&O Railroad.
- John Henry was not an ordinary man.
- The steam drill was introduced in the South in the 1870s.
- The story was popular in the South.

235

Hammering Out the Details

Cut out the hammers at the bottom of the page. Read each sentence. If the sentence tells something that happened in the story, glue a hammer in the box. Some hammers may be left over.

1. When John Henry left home, his mother gave him a book.

2. John Henry first saw Lucy Ann when he was getting a wagon out of the mud.

3. When John Henry was showing the boss he could drive steel, Little Bill held the spike for him.

4. John Henry didn't drive as much steel as the rest of the railroad crew.

5. In the contest, John Henry used two hammers at one time.

6. John Henry was in first place throughout the whole contest.

7. During the contest, the steam drill sputtered to a stop.

8. John Henry wanted to win the contest so the men could keep working.

237

A Hero's Story

A **legend** tells the story of a hero from the past. When the story is first told, it may be factual. As it is told again and again, parts of it grow larger than truth. This is called **exaggeration**.

Examples:
Events from the story that could really happen have pink squares. Exaggerated story events have blue squares.

- born during a thunderstorm
- learned to pick cotton when he was a little boy
- born with a hammer in his hand
- at age five, could pick as much cotton as two adults

Read the story events below. Choose your two favorite colors or patterns to complete the key. Then, use the key to color the squares. **Colors chosen will vary.**

Key

could really happen   exaggeration

- pulled a wagon out of the mud with one hand
- got a red kerchief from his mother
- helped a little girl find her kitten
- built a house, two barns, and a henhouse in one day
- worked for the railroad as a steel driver
- worked hard in hot weather

238

The Steel-Driving Man

Think about the character John Henry. Circle words in the following lists that describe him.

unique
popular
forgetful
driven
unkind
cranky

shy
hard worker
loyal
independent
foolish
imaginative

brave
determined
dishonest
helpful
dependable
ordinary

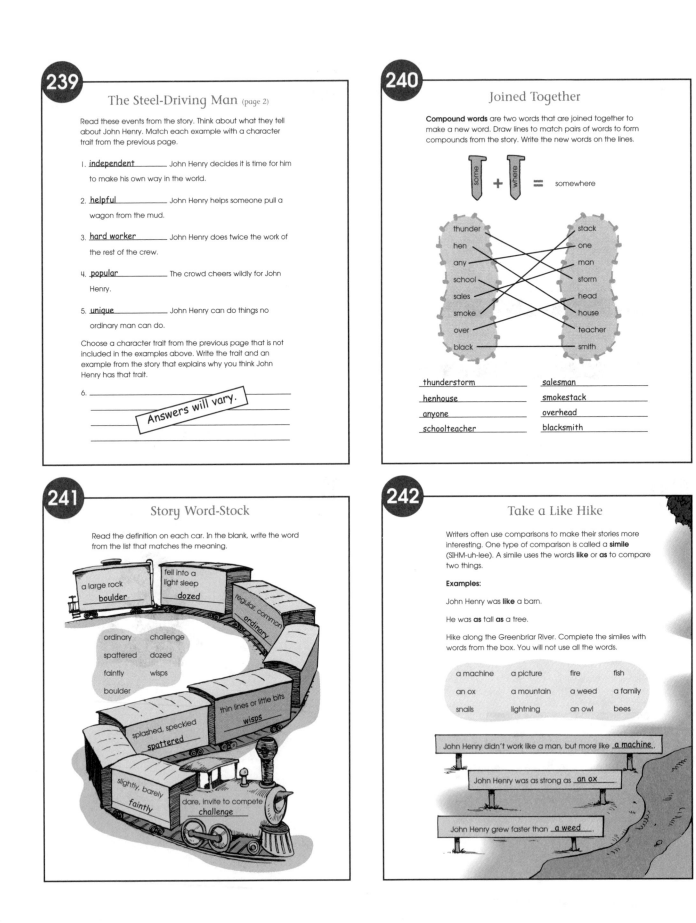

239

The Steel-Driving Man (page 2)

Read these events from the story. Think about what they tell about John Henry. Match each example with a character trait from the previous page.

1. <u>independent</u> John Henry decides it is time for him to make his own way in the world.

2. <u>helpful</u> John Henry helps someone pull a wagon from the mud.

3. <u>hard worker</u> John Henry does twice the work of the rest of the crew.

4. <u>popular</u> The crowd cheers wildly for John Henry.

5. <u>unique</u> John Henry can do things no ordinary man can do.

Choose a character trait from the previous page that is not included in the examples above. Write the trait and an example from the story that explains why you think John Henry has that trait.

6. _____

Answers will vary.

240

Joined Together

Compound words are two words that are joined together to make a new word. Draw lines to match pairs of words to form compounds from the story. Write the new words on the lines.

some + where = somewhere

thunder	stack
hen	one
any	man
school	storm
sales	head
smoke	house
over	teacher
black	smith

<u>thunderstorm</u>   <u>salesman</u>

<u>henhouse</u>   <u>smokestack</u>

<u>anyone</u>   <u>overhead</u>

<u>schoolteacher</u>   <u>blacksmith</u>

241

Story Word-Stock

Read the definition on each car. In the blank, write the word from the list that matches the meaning.

a large rock — <u>boulder</u>

fell into a light sleep — <u>dozed</u>

regular common — <u>ordinary</u>

ordinary	challenge
spattered	dozed
faintly	wisps
boulder	

thin lines or little bits — <u>wisps</u>

splashed, speckled — <u>spattered</u>

slightly, barely — <u>faintly</u>

dare, invite to compete — <u>challenge</u>

242

Take a Like Hike

Writers often use comparisons to make their stories more interesting. One type of comparison is called a **simile** (SIHM-uh-lee). A simile uses the words **like** or **as** to compare two things.

Examples:

John Henry was **like** a barn.

He was **as** tall **as** a tree.

Hike along the Greenbriar River. Complete the similes with words from the box. You will not use all the words.

a machine	a picture	fire	fish
an ox	a mountain	a weed	a family
snails	lightning	an owl	bees

John Henry didn't work like a man, but more like <u>a machine</u>

John Henry was as strong as <u>an ox</u>

John Henry grew faster than <u>a weed</u>

243

The crew was as busy as __bees__.

John Henry was built like __a mountain__.

The sun was as hot as __fire__.

The heat made the crew move as slowly as __snails__.

John Henry thought Lucy Ann was as pretty as __a picture__.

244

An Eyewitness Account

Pretend you are someone who watched the contest between John Henry and the steam drill. Complete each sentence.

That day of the contest between John Henry and the steam drill was _____

It all started when _____
_____
_____

I watched as John Henry _____
_____   *Answers will vary.*
_____

I couldn't believe it when _____
_____
_____

The most exciting moment was _____
_____
_____

I'll never forget that day because _____
_____
_____

245

Sign Up

Read the following poster advertising the contest between John Henry and the steam drill. Find and correct three capitalization mistakes, three punctuation mistakes, and two spelling mistakes. Make your corrections above each mistake or within the paragraph.

John
See man meet machine. ~~John~~ Henry will take

steam   June
on the ~~steem~~ drill. The contest will be ~~june~~ 5 ,

1872. It will begin at eight o'clock

The
in the morning. ~~the~~ stakes are high. If the

boss
steam drill wins, the ~~bose~~ has to buy it.

If John Henry wins, the crew continues

the work. Come cheer for John Henry.

280

Dare to Compare the Brothers

Read each phrase below. Decide if it describes Ali Baba or Cassim. Write the phrase in the space under the correct picture.

- can't keep a secret from his brother
- has help from a clever servant
- dies at the hands of the thieves
- shares the secret with his son
- wealthy merchant
- humble woodcutter
- overcome with greed
- forgets magic words

Ali Baba	Cassim
humble woodcutter	wealthy merchant
can't keep a secret from his brother	overcome with greed
has help from a clever servant	forgets magic words
shares the secret with his son	dies at the hands of the thieves

281

Sum of the Parts

Complete the chart below to tell about the different parts of the story "Ali Baba and the Forty Thieves."

Ali Baba and the Forty Thieves

Setting
long ago in Persia

Main Characters
Ali Baba, Cassim, Morgiana, captain of the thieves

Summary
Sample answer: Ali Baba discovers a cave full of riches that belongs to forty thieves. When he takes some of the treasure, the thieves want revenge. In the end, his clever servant Morgiana saves Ali Baba.

282

A Solution for Every Problem

Read and answer each question about how Morgiana solves problems in the story.

1. What did Morgiana do after the thieves marked Ali Baba's house with chalk to help them find it again later?
   She marked all the other houses nearby with chalk as well so they would all look the same.

2. What did Morgiana do when a thief asked from inside the oil jar, "Is it time yet?" Why?
   She answered, "Not yet, but soon," so the thief would think she was one of them. If she did not, the thieves would jump out and harm her.

3. Why did Morgiana roll the oil jars with the thieves in them down the hill?
   She did this to get rid of the thieves.

4. What did Morgiana do at the end of the story that saved Ali Baba's life?
   She recognized the captain of the thieves. She did a dance and used a dagger to drive him out of their lives forever.

283

Which Came First?

Cut out the sentence strips below. Use them to put the story events in order. Or glue each to the top of a half sheet of construction paper, and illustrate each page. Staple the pages together to make your own book.

1	Ali Baba goes to the forest to cut wood.
2	Ali Baba cannot believe his eyes when he sees what is inside the cave.
3	Cassim says, "Open, Barley!"
4	Morgiana puts chalk marks on other houses.
5	The captain drives up to Ali Baba's house in a cart filled with oil jars.
6	Morgiana rolls all the jars down a hill.
7	Morgiana figures out that their dinner guest is really the evil captain of the thieves.
8	The captain is driven away forever.
9	Ali Baba and his family live a safe and rich life.

285

Who Said That?

Read each sentence. Think about which character from the story might have spoken the words. Write the character's name to complete the sentence.

1. "One of you must go to the village. Find the one who knows too much," said __the captain__.

2. "I have saved us. You were entertaining the enemy," said __Morgiana__.

3. "If we use a little bit of gold at a time, no one will suspect our treasure," said __Ali Baba__.

4. "I demand to know what you measured with my scale!" said __Cassim__.

5. "Open, Barley!" shouted __Cassim__.

6. "I'll put a chalk mark on all the other houses to make them look the same," said __Morgiana__.

7. "At the signal, be ready to leap from your jars and attack," said __the captain__.

286

Clues to a Conclusion

Answer the following questions by drawing conclusions.

1. When the thieves first go into the cave, their saddlebags are full. When they come out, they are empty. Why?

   <u>The thieves have emptied them in the cave, adding</u>
   <u>more riches to the treasure.</u>

2. As Ali Baba watches the thieves, he makes sure he stays well hidden. Why?

   <u>If the thieves see him, they will hurt him because he</u>
   <u>knows about their treasure.</u>

3. When Cassim's body is gone the next day, the thieves figure something out. What?

   <u>They know that someone else took Cassim's body, so</u>
   <u>someone else must know about the treasure.</u>

4. Ali Baba says that Cassim's wife must be kept quiet about the way Cassim died. Why?

   <u>The thieves will figure out that the family knows</u>
   <u>about the treasure and will come after them, too.</u>

5. When Ali Baba realizes that Morgiana saved their lives, he asks if she wants to marry his son. Why?

   <u>He would like to have a clever daughter-in-law. He</u>
   <u>wants to show that he is grateful.</u>

287

Long Ago and Far Away in Persia

The **setting** of a story is the time and place in which a story happens. Think about the setting of "Ali Baba and the Forty Thieves." Read the list of places and things below. Circle the ones that belong in the setting for this story. Draw a line through those that don't belong.

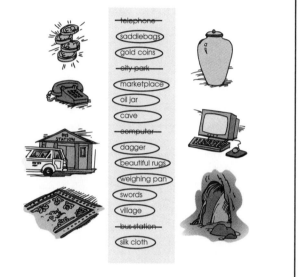

- ~~telephone~~
- saddlebags
- gold coins
- ~~city park~~
- marketplace
- oil jar
- cave
- ~~computer~~
- dagger
- beautiful rugs
- weighing pan
- swords
- village
- ~~bus station~~
- silk cloth

288

Tell Me All About It!

Adjectives are words that describe nouns. Adjectives tell what kind or how many. The words **a**, **an**, and **the** are special kinds of adjectives called articles that tell which one.

Examples:

what kind—**long** story

how many—**twenty** years

which one—**a** page

Read each sentence below. Circle each adjective in the sentence. There may be more than one in each sentence.

1. Cassim was (a) (greedy) man.
2. Ali Baba was (a) (lowly) woodcutter.
3. (A) (huge) rock covered (the) cave.
4. (The) captain said, "Open, sesame!" in (a) (deep) voice.
5. Ali Baba found (amazing) treasures.
6. Morgiana is (a) (clever) girl.
7. Ali Baba counted (forty) thieves near (the) (large) cave.

In number 7, which adjective tells which one? <u>the</u>

In number 7, which adjective tells how many? <u>forty</u>

In number 7, which adjective tells what kind? <u>large</u>

289

Say the Magic Words

Write the answer to each clue on the lines. Then, match the numbers, and use the letter above each number to fill in the answer to the riddle below.

The captain commanded forty of these <u>t h i e v e s</u>
                               2   7

Another word for weighing pan <u>s c a l e</u>
           11   8

It made the coin stick to the weighing pan <u>h o n e y</u>
                   9

Cassim was this to Ali Baba <u>b r o t h e r</u>
               6

Animals used for carrying heavy loads <u>d o n k e y s</u>
        10   1

How a thief marked Ali Baba's house <u>c h a l k</u>
          4

These didn't hold oil, but thieves <u>j a r s</u>
        3

The captain was disguised as this <u>m e r c h a n t</u>
       5

What does Ali Baba plant in his garden?
<u>S E S A M E</u> <u>S E E D S</u>
1 2 3 4 5 6   7 8 9 10 11

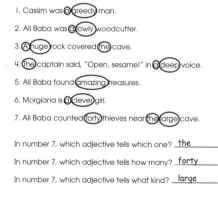

290

Treasure Map

Ali Baba has taken the treasure and buried it. Use the directions below to make a map on page 293 for Ali Baba to give to his son so he can find the treasure. Then, write out the directions to go from Ali Baba's house to the treasure.

Draw Ali Baba's house on the east side of the map.

Draw Cassim's house south of Ali Baba's house.

Draw some shops in the village west of the brothers' houses.

Draw the magic cave on the west side of the map.

Draw the forest surrounding the cave on the north, south, and east sides.

Draw some of the thieves east of the forest.

Now, make an **X** where you think Ali Baba might have hidden the treasure.

Directions from Ali Baba's house to the treasure:

Answers will vary.

291

Drawings will vary, but should be similar to what is shown. The treasure site marked with an X will vary.

Forest

Ali Baba's House

Thieves

Cave   Forest   Shops

Forest

Cassim's House

N
W   E
S

292

How Does the Story End?

What if Cassim had remembered the magic words and had been able to get out of the cave? What would have happened next? Use your imagination to write a new ending for the story in which Cassim escaped before the thieves returned. Draw a picture on another sheet of paper to illustrate your ending.

Answers will vary.

293

Sign Correction Time

Read the following sign the oil merchant might have written and look for mistakes. Find and correct three capitalization mistakes, three punctuation mistakes, and two spelling mistakes.

Omar
~~omar~~ the oil merchant will be in the
Wednesday
market next ~~wednesday.~~

Come early to buy your oil.

You
~~you~~ don't want to be in the dark.

oil
We have the best prices on ~~oyl~~

in the marketplace .

large
Look for the ~~larje~~ jars of oil.

Everyday Learning Activities

Learning can become an everyday experience for your child. The activities on the following pages can act as a springboard for learning. Some of the suggested activities may be used spontaneously as you are driving, shopping, or engaging in other everyday activities. Others are structured and require some readily available materials.

Reading and Speaking

Not Just Books With your child, explore all your local library has to offer. Look for a library calendar of special events, such as read-aloud times, puppet plays, and films. If you have a large library, make a special trip to check out nonbook materials such as CDs, videos, artwork, books on tape, and even games. While at the library, browse with your child through the collections of newspapers and magazines.

Reading Aloud Even though your child can read independently now, reading aloud and together is still a valuable activity. You can read books above the third grade reading level because children have a listening level higher than their reading level.

Why Do We Say It? Explore the origins of words and sayings by reading with your child books such as *Cat Got Your Tongue: The Real Meaning Behind Everyday Sayings* by Daniel Porter or *Settler Sayings* by Bobbie Kalman.

Twenty Questions Play Twenty Questions with your child, especially during "down times," such as commutes or while waiting in lines. One person begins by choosing an object without revealing what it is and identifying it for other players as animal, vegetable, or mineral. The other players then ask up to twenty questions about it in an effort to identify it. Questions can be answered only with *yes* or *no*.

Celebration Read-Alouds For holiday observances and other family celebrations, put your child in charge of selecting a passage that is fitting for the occasion. Have your child practice beforehand, so he or she can read aloud fluently at the big event. Your child may want to invite others to participate in the read-aloud as well.

Laughing at Language Share the silliness of language with your child. Look for books that contain tongue twisters, jokes, riddles, and jump-rope jingles. You might want to read these: *Anna Banana: 101 Jump-Rope Rhymes* by Joanna Cole, *Bennett Cerf's Book of Riddles* by Bennett Cerf, or *Busy Buzzing Bumblebees and Other Tongue Twisters* by Alvin Schwartz.

Quotation Montage Point out to your child an interesting quotation you come across. They are often found on calendars, in advertisements, in quotation dictionaries, and collections. Encourage your child to be on the lookout for quotations. He or she can jot down the most interesting quotations, using self-stick notes or whatever slips of paper are on hand. Remind him or her that it is important always to include the source. When your child has collected several that are related in some way or have special significance, he or she can make a montage of them in a notebook or other display and refer to it often.

Examples:

Reading is to the mind what exercise is to the body. —Joseph Addison

Nothing is a waste of time if you use the experience wisely. —Rodin

To climb steep hills requires slow pace at first. —William Shakespeare

If you're going to play the game properly, you'd better know every rule. —Barbara Jordan

Family Book Club From time to time, hold book discussions about a book everyone in the family has read. Make it a special time, serving simple snacks and beverages. You might want to develop a rating system for books, such as a point or star system. Encourage all members to share things they liked and disliked about the book, any questions they had, a comparison of the book with other books they have read, and whether they would like to read other works by the same author.

Writing

Predictions/Descriptions Choose a nearby place to visit that you and your child have never visited before. It might be a place of interest in your area, such as a historical site, museum, or park, or you might just want to make a change in your routine, such as visiting a different branch library. Before the visit, have your child write a description to predict what he or she thinks the place will look like. After the visit, have your child write an actual description. Together, compare the two descriptions.

Getting Directions When your family needs directions somewhere, ask your child to listen with you to the person giving directions and to make his or her own list. Before you begin the trip, read over your child's directions, and ask him or her for any clarification needed, consulting your own notes as necessary. Use a combination of your notes and your child's on the trip.

Title Twists You and your child can play a guessing game together, rewriting titles of familiar stories. Ask your child to make a list of book titles that are innovations, or twists, on the traditional. For example, *Through the Looking Glass* becomes *On the Other Side of the Mirror*. *Wind in the Willows* becomes *Breeze Through the Trees*. Make your own list, too, and take turns trying to identify the original versions of each other's titles.

Book Jacket Blurbs Have your child design a new book jacket for a favorite book. Have him or her write a brief summary (without giving away the ending). Encourage him or her to write a short review of the book on the flaps of the jacket.

Letters of Request When your child asks you for a privilege or object, ask him or her to put it in writing. Tell your child to write you a letter that clearly explains what he or she is asking for, including reasons for wanting this and why it is a good idea. Discuss the letter with your child, especially pointing out any of his or her reasons that were particularly persuasive.

Story by Mail Invite your child to begin a story that will be a collaborative effort. First, have him or her make a list of family members and friends to participate, being sure to include a few that live out of town. Help you child write a set of directions asking each person who receives the story to add to it and mail it to the next person on the list. When the story is completed, send everyone a copy of the completed version. This can be accomplished through regular mail or e-mail.

Critic at Large Encourage your child to write a review of a favorite toy, game, or musical recording. Remind him or her to be specific in telling why he or she likes it.

Math

Number Sense Hunt Try this number investigation activity in different places, such as at your home and in various stores. Ask your child to find objects that come in pairs, in dozens, in half dozens and other combinations, such as 16s or 24s. Have your child make a list of the objects and their groupings. For example, crayons may come in boxes of 24. Eggs come in dozens. Socks come in pairs.

Magic Square For a challenge, have your child draw a tic-tac-toe grid. Ask him or her to write the numerals 1 through 9 in the grid in such a way that no two rows, columns, or diagonals add up to the same number. Your child might also enjoy reading books with number puzzles, such as *Number Puzzles for Kids (Mensa)* by Harold Gale.

Flash Card Alternatives Instead of having your child say the answers when flashing the cards, have him or her say whether the answer will be odd or even. Give your child the entire deck of cards and have him or her sort the cards by the same answer. Or if you have flash card sets for several operations, have your child sort the cards into fact families, such as $2 \times 3 = 6$, $3 \times 2 = 6$, $6 \div 2 = 3$, $6 \div 3 = 2$.

Finally, have your child write a word problem or illustrate an equation from a flash card chosen randomly.

Letter to an Alien Suggest that your child write a letter to a space creature or an imaginary character, explaining a math concept he or she is learning. For example, your child might write about the characteristics of different three-dimensional shapes or about the concept of multiplication.

Personalized Problems Encourage your child to help you solve real-life mathematical problems you encounter, such as finding out how much money you will need to buy certain items at the grocery store. Ask, "If oranges are 4 for a dollar, how much money will we need to buy 6?"

Science

Daring Scientists Help your child make a list of types of scientists. See if you can name one for every letter of the alphabet. Then go to the library and check out books about some of them. You might want to try *Scientists: Their Lives and Works* by Peggy Saari or *Scientists Who Changed the World* by Philip Wilkinson. After your child reads a book, ask why he or she would or would not like to become that particular type of scientist.

Science All Around Plan a specific family science adventure with a visit to a science museum or zoo. With your child, read about related topics both before and after the event. You can turn almost any family outing into a scientific learning event. For example, even a trip to a water park could be enhanced by discussing the properties of water and the physics of slides.

Scientific Skills Encourage your child to develop the scientific skills of questioning, guessing, observing, testing, and drawing conclusions in everyday connections. Ask you child questions to help focus his or her thinking. For example, ask *What do you want to know?* or *What are you trying to find out?* to identify a problem. *What do you think might happen?* or *What do you know has happened in the past?* can help children make predictions. *What do you notice about it?* or *How does it look from different views?* can aid observations. *What does this tell us?* guides children in drawing conclusions.

Hands-On Science Do not wait until science-fair time to let your child do experiments at home. Many books feature experiments with materials that are probably available in your home. You may want to try *The Complete Book of Science, Grades 3–4*, McGraw-Hill Children's Publishing; *Janice VanCleave's Rocks and Minerals* by Janice VanCleave; *Science for Fun Experiments* by Gary Gibson; *356 Simple Science Experiments* by E. Richard Churchill, Louis V. Loeschnig, and Muriel Mandell; *Amazing Science Experiments with Everyday Materials* by E. Richard Churchill; or *Cool Chemistry: Great Experiments with Simple Stuff* by Steven W. Moje.

Social Studies

Bumper Stickers While traveling from one place to another, point out some bumper stickers and talk about their message. At home, encourage your child to draw and write some bumper stickers about social studies themes, such as citizenship or taking care of the Earth.

Great Americans Birthdays of great Americans are often well publicized in newspapers and on television. Help your child plan a family celebration of the contributions of some of these, even those that are not national holidays. Your child might want to read biographies of the "guest of honor" and make up games or other activities based on details from the person's life.

Multicultural Night With you child, explore a culture different from your own. Read books about the culture, and plan a night of fun that features food, music, crafts, and games you come across in your research.

Arts and Crafts

Signs of the Season You and your child can paint a seasonal design, perhaps one related to a holiday celebration. Use tempera paint, paintbrushes, and sponges to make the design.

Explore Fine Art Your child can take a look at a variety of artworks and learn a bit about the artists that created them by reading books such as *History of Art: The Guggenheim Museum Collection* by Marilyn J. S. Goodman, or any of the volumes of *Talking with Artists*, edited by Pat Cummings.

Story Plate Painting Many folk artists paint on dishware, sometimes even telling a story. Invite your child to "dish up" a story by painting on paper plates.

Giant Comic Strip Invite your child to use colored chalk to turn your driveway or sidewalk into a giant comic strip. If your child needs help with the subject of the strip, help him or her brainstorm interesting or amusing recent family events.

Notes